inside girl

LUCKY BREAK

girl

LUCKY BREAK

inside girl

a novel by **J. MINTER**

author of the insiders

BLOOMSBURY

NEW YORK BERLIN LONDON

BLOOMSBURY

Published by Bloomsbury U.S.A. Children's Books
175 Fifth Avenue, New York, NY 10010

Library of Congress Cataloging-in-Publication Data
Minter, J.
Lucky Break : an inside girl novel / by J. Minter. — 1st U.S. ed.
p.   cm.
Summary: Instead of the long-planned Spring Break trip to Paris with her friends, teenage
Flan, devastated after breaking up with her boyfriend Alex, finds herself traveling halfway
around the world trying to recover from her loss.
ISBN-13: 978-1-59990-356-9 • ISBN-10: 1-59990-356-3
[1. Interpersonal relations—Fiction. 2. Friendship—Fiction. 3. Voyages and travels—Fiction.]
I. Title.
PZ7.M67334Luc 2009   [Fic]—dc22   2008048794

alloy**entertainment**

Produced by Alloy Entertainment
151 West 26th Street, New York, NY 10001

First U.S. Edition 2009
Printed in the U.S.A. by Quebecor World Fairfield
10 9 8 7 6 5 4 3 2 1

for Harriet and Vic, with love

inside girl

LUCKY BREAK

*T*hey say springtime is for lovers. And when you're in love in the springtime, what better place to go than Paris? And who better to bring along to the City of Lights than four of your very best friends?

"Will my flatiron work with this adapter?"

"Do you think gladiator sandals are totally passé in Paris?"

"You guys are going to kill me—I forgot to renew my passport!"

"Girls," Camille commanded, waving her Phillip Lim bracelet cardigan–clad arms at our usual table in the crowded Thoney cafeteria. Everyone dropped her chopsticks to listen to my habitually calm, cool, and collected best friend say, "I can barely hear Flan think above all your stressing!"

"Sorry, Flan," Amory said, sliding her new pair of

black leather Antik Batik sandals back in their hemp shoe box. "What were you saying?"

"I wasn't saying anything," I realized. "Was I?"

"Not exactly," Camille admitted, twirling a strand of her signature waist-length dirty-blond hair around her finger. "But I know you, and you had that scheming little look on your face. Whenever you get that way, you're thinking about something important."

"Or . . . she's thinking about *Alex*," my other friend, Morgan, sang. It was kind of a new thing for Morgan to tease me for gushing about my boyfriend. Ever since she hooked up with her current beau, Bennett, I hardly recognized my previously romantically challenged pal. These days, Morgan always let her dark hair down, and more often than not, the girl formerly known as Little Miss Jaded wore pink.

Having been called out, I could feel my cheeks turn the shade of her fuchsia sweater.

"Oh, busted!" Camille joked.

"I wasn't *just* thinking about Alex," I defended myself. "I was thinking about all of us, being in Paris, *together*. Ladies, I have a feeling this spring break is going to be one for the books."

"Or the tabloids." Amory grinned. "Since I'm bringing a movie star," she sang, doing a seated version of the cabbage patch dance. "A movie star, movie star."

2

Camille threw her last piece of sushi at Amory. "Will you quit rubbing it in?" she teased. "And why are you so much better at the cabbage patch than me?"

After ducking to avoid getting smacked by sashimi, I grinned at my friends around the table. Following my brief but memorable era as a public school girl last fall, I'd been happily settling into the all-girl Thoney School on the Upper East Side. Not only was Thoney the alma mater of every female in my family, it was also the prep school of choice for my oldest friend, Camille. And, as she'd told me on the first day of school, when she introduced me to Harper, Amory, and Morgan: *mi posse es su posse*.

This posse had been planning our fabulous *voyage* for months, ever since the whole crew spent the night at my Perry Street town house for a classic movie night back in January. We'd rented *An American in Paris* and started out trying to one-up each other with our best impersonations of Leslie Caron pirouetting into Gene Kelly's arms. Well, one thing led to another, and the next thing we knew, I had the brilliant idea that we stop *acting* like Americans in Paris and *become* them. Except we didn't really want to stand out as *Americans*. The goal was to completely immerse ourselves in all things *français*.

The boy factor, well, that was a last-minute addition.

When Alex mentioned that he happened to be sans spring break plans, I had a revelation. It was just so rare that all five of us girls were simultaneously giddy over guys who returned the feeling. And what were the odds that all five of our crushes would be ready and willing to join us in Europe for ten days? I'd already found the most adorable flat on the Boulevard Saint-Germain, and the landlord just happened to have an identical suite for the boys on the floor directly below us. The vacation would be worlds away from the one I'd taken to Nevis with my Stuyvesant friends over Thanksgiving: all the stars were aligning for *this* trip to be unprecedentedly amazing.

I was almost shaking with excitement as I looked at the girls. There was Camille, already getting in the zone with her red velour beret. She'd confessed to having bought her boyfriend, Xander, a matching blue one at a sample sale on Broome Street—which had made Amory groan, but I assured her it would really bring out the intense blueness of Xander's eyes.

Morgan was gleefully texting Bennett, who was probably sitting in the Stuyvesant cafeteria down-town, editing his weekly column for the school news-paper while he waited for Morg's hourly check-in.

There was Amory, who I knew had bought the Antik Batik sandals because Jason James, her hottie actor crush, had mentioned that ancient Greek history was his favorite subject in school.

And there was Harper, who hadn't stopped wearing Lacoste tennis skirts over her Prada argyle tights ever since she started playing doubles with New York tennis legend Rick Fare.

We were all so freaking happy. So why were the girls staring at me with that anxious look in their eyes?

Oh, right—the trip planning! We were supposed to be going over last-minute details before our flight on Friday. We were supposed to be crossing the t's in our itinerary and dotting the i's in Paris with cute little hearts. Since the Golden Parisian Adventure (aka GPA) had been my idea in the first place, I'd kept up with most of the logistics in a massive golden binder that I'd found at a stoop sale on Stanton Street.

"Okay," I said, whipping out my binder. Jeez, this thing was getting heavy! "Where were we? Who forgot to renew her passport?"

"That would be me." Morgan raised her hand, looking sheepish.

"Not a problem," I said, making a note in the binder. "My mom's BFF with Chuck Schumer's travel coordinator. The senator programmed the embassy's phone number into her speed dial. E-mail me your social security number and I'll have them overnight it to you. Next?"

I looked up at my friends, who were staring at me with dropped jaws.

"What?" I asked.

"Flan, is that you?" Camille said. "You're so . . . *organized.*"

"Hey, don't sound so surprised," I said. "I can be organized. It just takes me being really, really, really excited about something. Like a romantic trip to *Paris* with all of you!"

"And don't think we don't appreciate your efforts with the doorstop—I mean, binder," Amory said, looking slightly intimidated by the size of the GPAB. "Any words of wisdom in there re the gladiator sandals?"

"They're adorable," I said.

"But do they say *Paris*?" Amory asked. "Or do they scream *tourist?*"

"Hmm, yes," Camille joked, lifting up a shoe by its long leather ankle strap. "All you need now is a fanny pack and an over-the-shoulder camera."

Jokes aside, I knew Amory was serious about her trends. She'd be mortified if she were spotted on the Rive Gauche wearing something gauche.

"Hold up the shoes," I told her. I picked up my iPhone and snapped a picture of A holding the sandals with a nervous little smile. Then I texted it to my friend Jade Moodswing, the be-all and end-all of French fashion.

CHIC OU PAS CHIC? I wrote.

A minute later, her response:

TRÈS, TRÈS CHIC!

I held out the phone for Amory to read.

"Thanks, Flan!" She beamed. "Huge sigh of relief."

"Moving on," I said, checking that off my list. "Someone had a question about a hair straightener?"

Dutifully, Harper produced her don't-leave-home-without-it flatiron, which we'd dubbed the Blue Genie for its deep aquamarine hue and magical defrizzing capabilities. In her other hand she held out an adapter that looked like it had been purchased in 1983.

"Yikes," I said. "I wouldn't trust anything I loved with that monstrosity. Short-circuit city. Here," I continued, pulling out a small, sleek adapter that I'd borrowed from my sister's stash. Feb had an adapter for just about every place on earth that used electricity. "Use this."

Harper pitched the older model into the trash with a hefty thud.

"Thanks." She smiled. "This will be much easier to fit in my carry-on!"

"Such a little troop leader, Flan." Camille laughed.

She'd known me since elementary school, so she did have a right to be surprised. Just last month, I'd gotten myself in *way* over my head when I tried to set up *all* my friends on blind dates on the same night. And then there was that time when I thought I could single-handedly redesign the school's démodé lacrosse uniforms as the platform when I ran for class office.

Somehow, I always managed to pull off my crazy schemes in the end, but as my partner in crime, Camille had witnessed many a plan B, plan C . . . and sometimes a plan D before I spelled success.

"What else do you have in that carpetbag?" she asked, pointing at my Chloé taupe messenger. "Toilet paper? Girl Scout cookies?"

"Rope?"

Our whole table looked up to see Kennedy Pearson and Willa Rubenstein standing over us, hands on both of their hips.

Kennedy had just gotten a short Katie Holmes blunt cut that only made her look more like the angry Doberman she was. She still wasn't over the fact that I had friends because I was nice. And Willa, with her million-dollar wardrobe practically falling off her waif figure . . . well, none of us had ever really been able to figure out what Willa's problem was—

other than being friends with Kennedy, the devil incarnate.

"Okay, Kennedy." I sighed. "I'll play along. Why would I need rope exactly?"

Kennedy shrugged. "Only because I heard that you had to bribe your so-called boyfriends to come with you on this little trip. Since they'll probably run screaming from you as soon as the plane touches down in Paris, you might want to bring some rope, you know, to keep them on a tight leash."

Our entire table busted out laughing, much to Kennedy's infuriation. What made it so hilarious was the fact that Kennedy used to have this power over me. A comment like that back in seventh grade would have sent me sobbing into the bathroom. But by now, I knew who I was. And I also knew who Kennedy was: a fading star who would lie her way back to being popular if she thought she had a chance.

"And what are you doing over spring break, Kennedy?" Amory asked. "Nursing Willa back to health after her third nose job?"

"Or starring in an episode of *What Not to Wear*?" Camille added.

But Kennedy didn't take her eyes off me.

"'Bye, Kennedy," I said, waving to give them both the hint. "Whatever you end up doing over spring break, I hope you have *almost* as much fun as we're going to have." I looked back at the girls. "Like that's possible."

"A hundred dollars says everything falls apart before your flight even takes off," Willa hissed, rolling her eyes once more before she and Kennedy stormed out of the cafeteria.

"So, who wants the last bite of my croissant?" Camille asked once they were gone, because we were *so* over wasting our time acknowledging those two.

"Me!" the rest of us all shouted together, fighting for the crusty end piece.

"You know," Harper said, looking at her platinum Movado watch. "In a little less than, oh, seventy-two hours, we won't have to fight over the last bite of croissant." She grinned around the table.

"Because we'll be . . ." Amory sang, reviving her cabbage patch dance.

"In Paris!" we all shouted together, collapsing on the table in a fit of excited laughter.

After school, I swung by my trusty tailor, Mrs. Woo, to pick up the yellow Miu Miu cocktail dress I'd had altered.

When I walked into her tiny underground shop on Jane Street, Mrs. Woo dropped the pair of AG jeans she was hemming and started waving her arms in the air. She dashed to the back room, emerging a minute later with my ray-of-sunshine dress hanging in a plastic bag. My mom had sworn by Mrs. Woo since Feb was wearing Ralph Lauren Baby. She pretty much knew our family's inseams inside and out.

"You'll wear this to fancy Flood family dinner tonight?" she asked.

"No," I said, holding the strapless knee-length dress up against me in the mirror. I couldn't wait to get it on. "I'm going to a party with my boyfriend. It's

11

a benefit for a charity resort opening in Maui, so I thought, you know, yellow . . . sunlight . . ."

"Perfect." Mrs. Woo nodded, closing her eyes. "But your mother will miss you tonight. She came by this morning to pick up the St. John suit for the dinner party."

"No," I said, confused. "My parents are in Minsk—"

Just then, my phone rang. I looked at the screen and saw my mother's photo pop up. It was one I'd snapped of her lying on our living room couch with two cucumber slices over her eyes. She'd kill me if she knew I'd taken it—usually Mom insisted on striking a pose—but this image was my favorite way to imagine her: close to home.

I flashed the phone at Mrs. Woo, smiled, and said, "Guess I should take this. Thanks for the dress!" Stepping back out on the street with the dress draped over my arm, I picked up the phone.

"How quickly can you be at Morimoto?" my mom said.

"Huh? I'm supposed to meet Alex at 60 Thompson in an hour. I didn't even know you were—"

"In town?" my mom finished. "Don't remind me. Long story short—the plane ran out of fuel halfway to Minsk. We're here for one night before we jet to the

Amalfi Coast. But it's not all bad, darling. Patch and Feb are here too. We've all got scads to go over before we take off again." My head was spinning, but Mom was still going a mile a minute. "Your father and I figured the most painless way to iron out logistics would be over family dinner. It'll be half organizational, half show-and-tell, entirely delicious. So you'll meet us? Mori's working tonight so he'll do a special menu."

I didn't need Morimoto's touch to seal the deal—though I was obsessed with his scallop sashimi salad. Usually, when someone in my family told me to jump, I did: right into a cab to meet them. But what was I going to tell Alex?

"Do you want to invite the Prince?" Mom sang.

Among my friends, Alex had earned his nickname—the Prince of New York—back in my huge-crush days, when I was still intimidated by his cool demeanor at parties. Ever since she overheard me call him that on the phone with Camille one day, my young-at-heart mom hadn't been able to let go of the nickname.

I knew that Alex had been looking forward to this party for weeks. Some of his lacrosse friends from D.C. were taking the train up, and he hardly ever got to see them.

"You know what?" I said to my mom. "Alex will understand. We're spending ten days with each other in Paris anyway. I'll meet you guys at the restaurant in twenty."

Hailing another cab and wondering whether the yellow dress would be too much for a family dinner—who was I kidding? I was a Flood!—I texted Alex.

HEY, BABE. MOM SURPRISED ME WITH A FAMILY DINNER THAT WOULD BE HARD TO MISS. FORGIVE ME FOR SKIPPING THE PARTY TONIGHT?

He wrote back:

ONLY IF YOU PROMISE TO SIT NEXT TO ME ON THE PLANE. GIVE MY REGARDS TO LES FLOODS.

Awesome. I hopped out of the cab feeling lucky that Alex and I never had to deal with drama. We were both just naturally understanding and trusting and laid back. I ducked into the bathroom in the Chelsea Market across the street to change into my dress. Zipping it up, I looked in the mirror and was blown away once again by Mrs. Woo's needlework. The crisp puff of the skirt hugged my hips, and she'd taken in the once-gaping bust so that it lay across my skin just perfectly. I ran my fingers through my long blond hair and dotted on my sheer peony Stila lip gloss.

I looked at my watch—good, I was still in the realm of fashionably late. I crossed the street and pulled open the heavy glass door of Morimoto.

The Japanese restaurant was immaculately clean

and spare, with sleek draped white ceilings, bamboo banquettes, and transparent paneled walls with about a million shimmering blue lightbulbs behind them. When you breathed in, you couldn't smell anything— which was unusual for a restaurant, but the best indicator of superfresh sushi. The dining room was so quiet that the waiters were actually whispering.

It was all so Zen—and so *not* Flood. I guessed my family wasn't here yet. If they had been, I'd have heard them.

Someone tapped my shoulder. I turned around to face a hostess in a sleek white silk kimono. "Are you Flan Flood?" she whispered.

"Yes," I whispered back, feeling funny.

"Your family reserved the private den in the back." She pointed toward a beaded curtain and I followed her down a dimly lit hallway. When she opened the door to the private den I never knew existed, I suddenly felt right at home.

The room was bustling, loud, full of color—and more than a few people who I was pretty sure weren't in my family.

"There she is!" My dad beamed, stepping forward to give me a hug. Dad's face was glowing, probably from the golf tournament he'd played last week in Caracas, and his eyes were twinkling—probably from having his entire family in the same room for a change.

"Hi, Dad." I gave him a kiss. "So Minsk was a no-go?" I couldn't remember what my professionally globe-trotting parents were up to in Minsk, but if my dad had anything to say about it, the trip was probably related to his crazy real estate adventures.

"Between you and me," Dad whispered, "I'd much rather go straight to Amalfi. You can't beat the burrata down there. Melts in your mouth. But don't bring it up to your mother. She's all touchy because she was supposed to lunch with Putin's wife in Minsk. Grab a seat—they're filling up fast."

"Okay, but uh, who are all these people?" I asked. I was used to seeing my parents' assistants dashing in and out of our house on the rare occasion when Mom and Dad graced our brownstone with their presence . . . but this much help seemed excessive even for my parents.

"What, you didn't bring your personal assistant?" My older brother, Patch, appeared out of nowhere to pull my hair, which he did every single time he saw me—whether or not I was sporting an expensively blown-out updo. Luckily, today, it didn't mess up my no-fuss look.

"Seriously?" I asked, looking around. In the mayhem

of the private dining room, I recognized my mom's personal assistant, Leora. She never left the house without something leopard print, and today was no exception. A big head scarf *and* suede high heels—a bold move.

But I didn't recognize the guy next to her in the tweed three-piece suit and the retro bowl cut—or the redheaded twins sitting across the table from my sister, Feb, who'd dyed her hair a similar shade of red. Feb was wearing a simple brown slip dress that looked like it could have been made of burlap, and all three of them were looking down at a very big calculator.

"Well, you know Leora, of course," Patch gestured. "Tweed Man is Dad's assistant on the Amalfi deal, forget his name. And the Double Trouble tête-à-tête with Feb, they're some sort of animal rights activist cohorts or something. If I were you, I would not get them talking about the earth-friendly henna dye they used to get that hair."

Leave it to Patch to explain my family's craziness with so much nonchalance that we almost seemed normal.

"And where's your PA?" I asked him, jokingly. Hiring an assistant was so not my brother's style.

Patch rolled his eyes and pointed behind him to where his girlfriend, Agnes, was barking orders at a cowering blond girl with a notebook.

"I try to stay out of it." Patch shrugged. "What about you, little sis? You didn't bring your own trip planner? Word is you're off to gay Paree . . . with Alex?"

"Yeah." I grinned. "But all my friends are coming too, and actually, I planned it by myself. We're renting a couple little flats on the Seine that I found online. I have our whole itinerary right here." I started to pull out the GPA binder, but it was so heavy, I opted for just pointing at it.

Patch blinked at me a few times. "You did all that yourself?" he asked. "Impressive."

"This meeting will now come to order," Leora boomed. Someone had wheeled in a podium and a microphone. A projector screen lowered behind her.

"Wait," I heard my mother shriek. "No one told me Flan arrived—or that she looked so spectacular in her dress!" Mom darted over to me and planted a big kiss on my cheek. "Hi, darling. So glad you're here." She looked up. "Leora, carry on!"

On command, Leora recommenced, and the dinner party ran in a remarkably organized manner. There was a PowerPoint show detailing my parents' vacation—it was a *vacation*, Mom kept interrupting to insist, pointing at my father, meaning *no BlackBerries*!

Then there was a short video that Feb's PAs had

come up with to go over her upcoming trip to Bangkok. The plan was for Feb and her boyfriend, Kelly, to spend three months helping the locals sow organic rice fields. It looked more like a Peace Corps advertisement than anything else, but it also looked really cool and unique. Feb's face lit up as she watched it. Clearly she was totally psyched to get over there and get her hands . . . uh . . . ricey.

In between presentations, Morimoto stopped in to say hello and to offer us a palate cleanser. The look on his face when he saw our dinner party, board meeting style, was priceless. He was so stunned, he nearly dropped his tray of lychee-cucumber sorbet.

After we'd palate-cleansed, Agnes shoved her terrified PA to the podium to present the slide show of Patch and Agnes's Superchill Aussie Bonfire Experience. Patch's face lit up at the pictures of all the partying on the beach, but I had to laugh at Agnes's very detail-oriented schedule: wake up, 7:05; breakfast on the terrace, 7:15; and so on.

And just before dessert, my mom got up on the podium and said, "Flan, would you like to tell us anything about your trip?" She squeezed Leora's hand and bragged, "Flan's going to Paris with the Prince of New York!"

Leora, who must have been used to my mom

gushing about things no one else understood, just nodded her approval.

I looked around at the full house, suddenly aware that I was going up there solo—no presentation, no PA to fall back on. I heaved my binder out of my bag. But once I got up there, I realized I didn't even need it. I knew all the details by heart.

By the time I gave my five-minute spiel about all the amazing sights we were going to see, food we were going to eat, and clothes we were going to buy, I was really revved up about the trip.

"Who'd you use, Flan?" Agnes called from her seat. "I mean, to help you plan?"

"No one," I stammered. "I planned it myself. I read a couple guidebooks and Googled some stuff."

For a second, I wondered if maybe I'd been careless about this. Should I have outsourced some help? But then, led by Patch, my entire family rose and gave me a standing ovation.

"Marvelous, darling," my mom gushed, tears in her eyes. "Just promise me one thing?"

I nodded, waiting for her to go on.

"That you'll wear that gorgeous dress at the top of the Eiffel Tower with the Prince of New York—and e-mail it to me in Sorrento!"

"Done and done." I laughed.

Chapter 3

*A*fter French class the next day, I skipped out on the faux French onion soup in the Thoney cafeteria and met my French-manicured sister at the Upper East Side's premier French brasserie, Orsay.

It's sort of an unspoken rite of passage for a girl to be taken to Orsay by her mother when she reaches a "certain age" in New York. With its old-style brass Parisian bar, supertraditional French menu, and classy dark green leather booths, Orsay is definitely not a place for children (though I'm sure more than a few stroller-wielding, salade niçoise–munching Upper East Side mothers would disagree).

The food is always sophisticated and precise, though often an acquired taste. I'll never forget when my mother took me to Orsay for frog legs the day I first got my period, because "I was a woman now and needed to be able to handle things that might initially

21

not be to my taste." Plus, she told me—*and*, to my utter horror, the waiter—nothing combated a bad case of menstrual cramps like a nice crispy order of *cuisses de grenouille*.

Once I got over the mortification of having the whole restaurant overhear her, I actually kind of got into the frog legs. They really do taste like chicken! Plus, as Camille later told me, it could have been worse: when she got her period, her half-Jewish grandmother slapped her across the face, because that was what they did in the old country to welcome a girl to the harsh realities of womanhood. Yikes.

Today, when I crossed Lexington Avenue toward Orsay's outside patio lined with overflowing planters, I decided to pass on the frog legs. It was one of those rare sunny mid-March afternoons in Manhattan, where there was *almost* a hint of warmth in the air, and my plan was to celebrate the advent of spring with the famous Orsay spring salad, topped with a crusty roulette of sautéed goat cheese.

Feb was seated with her back to Lexington, but I could still spot her a mile away. Her massive black Dior sunglasses were perched atop her head, and she was typing madly on her BlackBerry (a trait I know she must have inherited from my father). Even though Feb had "gone granola" (as Patch liked to say) when she met her boyfriend, Kelly, a few months ago, there were still a couple things from her former city life that she hadn't given up.

"Bonjour, Feb," I said, kissing her high cheekbone as the black-suited waiter pulled out my chair.

"Coo-coo, *chérie*," Feb said, turning her face to accept my kiss without even looking up from her PDA screen. "Two minutes and I'm all yours."

"Can I get you something to drink, mademoiselle?" the waiter asked me, his pad and pen at the ready.

"How about a cappuccino?" I said.

Feb's head shot up. "Uh-uh." She shook her finger at me. "Cappuccino is for *after* the meal, to be drunk slowly, over dessert."

"Feb, I only have fifty-five minutes before I have to be back for chemistry. I don't know about all these courses—"

"Flan." She sighed. "You'll be in Paris in two days. You really need to start adjusting your relationship with time. The French would never confine a good meal to a time-crunch just because of some boring class." She turned to the waiter. "She'll start with a Pellegrino now, and cappuccino later."

I looked at the waiter, whose shrug told me that my sister spoke the truth about the French rules and orders of beverage consumption.

I shrugged back. You didn't have to ask me to twice to skip chemistry. Slowly enjoying my cappuccino over dessert it was!

"So," she said, finally putting down her BlackBerry. "All packed up?"

For my sister, who, like the rest of my family, never really stayed anywhere long enough to *un*pack, being "all packed up" was pretty much just her general state of affairs. For me, however, who *hated* to pack (how was I supposed to know what I'd feel like wearing six days from now?), packing was almost always put off until the very last minute.

I shook my head meekly, knowing what was coming from my occasionally tyrannical big sister.

Feb stared at me. "Well, have you done *anything* to prepare? Do you have your adapter and your passport ready? Do you even know what the weather is going to be like over there? It sounds like you need help getting organized." She sighed. "Do I need to lend you Lena and Laura for the day?"

"Hey," I said. "Give me a little credit. Didn't you hear my presentation last night at dinner?" For an off-the-cuff speech, I thought I'd presented my plans very well. Why was Feb giving me such a hard time?

"Sorry," she said, "I had to step out at dinner to take a call from Kelly. He's all worked up about the water level in the rice paddies in Bangkok. The monsoons have been underwhelming this season." She paused. "Sorry, boring. Anyway, I had to talk him off the ledge. Why don't you give me a refresher course?"

I sighed, heaving the GPA binder out yet again. Feb's eyes widened when she saw the size of it, but they lit up when I started flipping through the pages. She nodded approvingly at the image printouts of our matching flats on the Boulevard Saint-Germain, and the Métro route I'd already mapped out for us to take to the Champs-Elysées.

"*Magnifique.*" She clapped when I'd finished. "Well, I guess I should eat my words—after I finish these oysters. You've really got a handle on your little Parisian adventure."

"*Golden* Parisian Adventure," I corrected, as the waiter set down our main course.

Feb gave me a mischievous smile and waved a sheet of paper in the air. "Then I guess you don't even need the list of tips that Jade Moodswing and I prepared for you—"

"Hey, let me see that!" I threw down my fork. The goat cheese could wait—I definitely wanted in on the latest Parisian scoop from Feb and Jade.

"Okay, good," Feb said, sounding happy to be needed again. "Keep that binder handy so you can take notes. You must, must, must go to Café du Marché on rue Cler for lunch; then there's Angelina's after the Louvre for hot chocolate, and of course Aubergine for the fizziest juices you've ever tasted." She looked up from her list. "Can Alex dance?"

"That's like asking if the French make wine," I said, remembering when Alex had hired a private tango instructor for us on Valentine's Day—and proceeded to put me to shame with his moves. "The boy practically invented it."

"Good." Feb nodded. "Then you'll go to Étoile. It gets really good after about three a.m." She looked wistful for a second. "God, I miss Paris," she said. Then she shook her head and the nostalgia seemed to vanish. "You're just going to have to go all out so I can live vicariously through you, okay?"

"Promise," I said. With these tips from Feb, there was little chance of our crew *not* going all out. I couldn't wait to pass along these latest itinerary additions to my friends.

"What else do I need to know?" I asked. "I've already been warned about my embarrassing tendency to prematurely order cappuccino. And I texted Jade yesterday to get her French thumbs-up on a pair of sandals that my friend Amory just bought at Bendel's—"

"Perfect." Feb nodded. "I was just getting to fashion. Now, I haven't been to Paris in at least three weeks, so I did have to lean on Jade a little bit more in that department. French restaurants are timeless—not at all like New York—but *like* New York, the look on the street changes every day." She consulted her list. "Here's what Jade says everyone is wearing, as of three-fifteen Paris time today: cigarette pants with billowy shirts and tiny men's vests. You could do plaid, or cable knit, or even argyle." She read down the list from Jade. "Nighttime is another story—everything has gone up, up, up in formality. You're going to need some gowns."

All the advice from Feb and Jade was priceless, but it was also starting to make me a feel a little frantic. We were leaving tomorrow—was I supposed to tell all my friends to run out and buy argyle vests tonight?

"Okay," Feb said. "I can see from the way you're biting that little bottom lip of yours that you're freaking."

I grimaced—Feb had an uncanny way of reading me.

"*N'inquiétes pas, ma soeur*," she assured me. "Jade Moodswing has graciously insisted that you bring your friends to her atelier after you sleep off the jet lag. She'll outfit you with the latest fashions. That way, you won't even be one day out of style."

My eyes widened and I gripped Feb's hand across the table.

"Bring the boys too." She shrugged. "You know she's just starting to branch into menswear. She'll be happy for a few studly American models. Okay, Flan," she said. "I know you're excited, but you're going to have to stop waving my hand in the air like that. People are starting to stare."

Whoops. I hadn't realized that my enthusiasm was causing such a scene. If Feb thought *I* was energetic, she should be there when I told my friends we'd be making a cameo at a real-life French atelier.

The waiter came by to clear our plates and said, "You still want the cappuccino, mademoiselle? Or maybe you have already had enough caffeine *aujourd'hui*?"

Feb laughed under her breath, and when I insisted that I could handle the caffeine without another embarrassing outburst of energy, we ordered the chocolate soufflé so that our savoring could linger on a little longer.

So what if it was halfway through my next class already? When you were getting too-rare bonding time and travel tips from your big sister, who cared about the periodic table?

"Thanks, Feb," I said. "I know you're busy with your Thailand planning, and—"

"Please." Feb waved her hand dismissively, never one to get too mushy. "Don't flatter me. I feel like I should do more. I mean, it's your first time in Paris with your boyfriend." She grinned. "Which reminds me. I've given you fashion advice, and I've given you restaurant suggestions." She tapped her finger to her temple. "What else am I forgetting? My little sister's going to the romance capital of the world—voilà!" she said dramatically. "You must need some romance advice, *oui*?"

"*Non*." I grinned, crossing my arms over my chest and trying to look coyly French. "Luckily, things with Alex are so great, romance is the one area I definitely don't need any advice!"

aging Ms. Flannery Flood to Women's Sportswear. Ms. Flannery Flood," the Saks Fifth Avenue intercom boomed. I'd just spun through the doors on the ground floor of the bustling department store for a shopping date with my best friend/teen starlet, Sara-Beth Benny. Both of us needed some last-minute pre–spring break essentials.

Apparently, much of Manhattan had the same idea. The cosmetics department was jammed with girls and women of all ages and credit limits, suddenly in need of SPF foundation, skin-firming body lotion, and shimmery beach-proof lip gloss. Walking through all the commotion, I was relieved to have much of the shopping pressure lifted off my shoulders by Jade Moodswing's gracious offer to provide some fabulous Frenchie clothes. But from the tone of

SBB's thirteen texts since lunch—and the urgent intercom summons—my movie star friend was in an altogether different state.

SBB had just gotten the lead in an as-yet-untitled megablockbuster, but she'd been hesitant to spill any of the details. Until the official press release went out, the film was *so* under wraps that SBB was sure her phone was being tapped by the rampant paparazzi. She insisted on waiting until we met in person to fill me in, only stressing cryptically that the part was going to be "a real growing experience" for her.

The elevator spit me out on the fifth floor just as the intercom clicked on again and I heard the beginning of my page: "Ms. Flannery Flood to the—"

"Here I am," I called loudly at the speaker on the ceiling, earning confused looks from a few nearby shoppers. "I'm coming as fast as I—"

"You're Flannery Flood." A sales assistant grabbed my wrist. She was pretty, with dark skin and bright pink lipstick, but underneath the expensively made-up face, there was worry. "You've got to hurry."

I was used to SBB's little shopping freak-outs—we'd done calming yogic breathing sessions in most of the dressing rooms in Manhattan—so I had to laugh at this girl's panic. But I let her pull me toward the back of the floor where I could already vaguely hear the shrieks of my high-strung friend.

When the sales assistant zipped me past the Marc Jacobs dressing room, where SBB liked to try on clothes because it offered the most privacy and best mirrors, I paused.

"She's not in there?" I pointed. "That's her usual—"

"Keep going," she ordered, pulling me all the way back toward the windows looking down on Fifth Avenue. What were we doing in the athletic-wear section?

"She's in there," the salesgirl said, but by then, I'd already heard the telltale thumps of SBB wreaking havoc on the dressing room. I nodded thanks at my escort and stepped cautiously inside the danger zone.

SBB was drowning in a sea of Stella McCartney running pants, zip-up Juicy sweatshirts, and high-end spandex. She was wearing leggings and a sports bra that looked like they were made out of titanium alloy.

"And what are you wearing, Ms. Benny?" I stepped forward, dramatically mimicking a red-carpet interviewer with a microphone. "Don't tell me—was that outfit designed by . . . NASA?"

SBB crossed her arms over her chest. "You are the

only person on the *planet* I could forgive for making a joke at a time like this."

"With that outfit," I said, "you could probably go into orbit and make friends with a few comedians on other planets."

Finally, I got a tiny smile out of my tiny friend. "Thank God you're here." She sighed.

"Where's Shay?" I asked. Shay was SBB's personal shopper. She had a tough, no-nonsense exterior that had sent more than a few shopgirls running for the hills, but when they weren't catfighting, Shay and SBB worked really well together. I assumed in a fashion emergency such as this one—whatever it was—SBB would already have called in all the reinforcements on her contacts list.

SBB shook her head. "That big-mouthed know-it-all couldn't keep her piehole shut long enough to make it out of this store. I can't trust her with something like *this*." She turned around and pointed to the series of clasps on the sports bra. "Now help me get out of this trap."

"Only if you finally tell me what this is all about," I said, freeing her from the aerodynamically designed athletic wear.

When she was comfortably changed into a loose-fitting gray Theory tank and pajama pants, SBB took a good look around the dressing room, got up on a step stool to turn off a camera over our heads—"in case anyone at the security desk can read lips"—and motioned for me to sit down next to her.

I pushed aside the mountain of tracksuits and took a seat.

"Okay, formalities first: pinky swear your lips are sealed. I mean, I know you're good for it, but—"

I stuck out my pinky to nip her lengthy apology in the bud. "Pinky swear," I said.

SBB took a deep breath and said, "Well, it's finally happening."

From her tone, I felt like I was supposed to know what she meant—as if "it" were the world's only inevitability. I nodded, trying to look like I was keeping up with her.

"JR is making his directorial debut," she said slowly, and very proudly.

JR—Jake Riverdale—was SBB's boyfriend, and the biggest pop star–turned–movie star (turning director) in L.A. Scratch that—in the world. He and SBB were an amazing match—in fact, they were so unwaveringly supportive of each other's skyrocketing careers that they were famous in the tabloids for being Hollywood's most likely to succeed couple.

"That's so exciting, SBB," I said, leaning in to give her a hug.

"There's a catch," she said gravely. "He wants me cast as the lead."

"What a jerk," I joked. "Come on, SBB. Isn't that some sort of Hollywood pinnacle? You guys might be the youngest couple in history to have that kind of sway."

SBB buried her face in a mound of sports bras. "Not when *everyone* in the industry is expecting me to fail," her muffled voice wailed.

"SBB," I said, "why would anyone expect you to fail?"

She leaned in and lowered her voice. "The film is called *Gladiatrix*. I have to battle *lions*. They need me to gain half my body weight in muscle. What if . . ." Her eyes grew terrified. "What if I can't cut it?"

So that explained all the athletic gear splayed out around us. SBB was about as aerobically challenged as I was. (Once we'd put on my mother's cardio-Pilates video in our home theater, only to make it through the warm-up before collapsing on the beanbag chairs with a big bag of kettle corn.) It almost made sense that she thought she could shop her way into the role of a gladiatrix. I put my hand on her knee.

"SBB, I've seen you go from your city girl self to a

singing Bonnie and Clyde, to a French foreign exchange student, to a Moroccan heiress, all without batting a cat eye. You can act any part you put your mind to."

SBB turned her lip down. "Really?" she squeaked.

"What you need is a trainer, maybe one or two sets of workout clothes"—I picked up the scarily heavy silver sports bra—"and to forget this thing ever existed."

SBB threw her arms around me—always the key sign that I'd successfully calmed her down. "Oh, Flannie." She sighed. "What would I do without you? Gosh—trying on all that heavy sportswear really worked up my appetite. Want to grab a milk shake upstairs? JR says now I can eat anything I want, as long as I sprinkle a half a cup of protein powder in it." She reached into her purse and waved a Ziploc bag of beige powder in the air.

"Okay, that's nasty." I laughed. "But you know I never say no to a milk shake."

SBB paid for a comfy pale lavender Theory tracksuit and we took the elevator to the top floor toward the airy white café, Snacks at Saks.

"Well," SBB said, sidling through the crowded restaurant to look for a table. "Now that my spaz attack is over, let's talk about your fabulously romantic spring break trip to Paris, shall we?" Her head whipped around. "Oh my God, Amber! What are you doing here?"

SBB leaned down to air-kiss a beautiful dark-haired girl eating a seaweed salad at the bar. I recognized her as Amber Mobley, SBB's costar from the romantic country-and-western comedy *Holding Merle Haggard*.

"I'm in between sets," Amber said, accepting the kiss. "So I flew out to visit an old friend. Do you and your friend want to join us for dinner?" She turned to me, smiled, and stuck out her hand. "I'm Amber."

SBB put her hand on my shoulder. "This is my very best friend," she said proudly. "Flan Flood."

Amber's eyes narrowed and she made a very small "huh" noise under her breath. What was that about? It was almost like the sound of my name surprised her. But before I had the chance to ask, I felt a tap on my shoulder.

"Oh, hi, Flan. What brings *you* to *our* table?"

It was Kennedy Pearson. She slid into the seat across from Amber and jerked her thumb at me. "This is the girl I was just telling you about." She looked back at me. "We were all at this party at 60 Thompson last night, maybe you heard about it. A benefit for the Maui Hotel."

That was the party Alex went to last night. The party I skipped because of my family dinner.

"It was so fun," Kennedy continued, something in her voice sounding suspiciously excited. "And so many cute boys there." She winked at Amber. "Oh my God, I'll show you guys pictures."

SBB and I glanced at each other warily. It wasn't like Kennedy to delve into party details with me.

She whipped out her iPhone and started scrolling through her pictures from the night before. "Here's one of Amber getting hit on by Leo, and here's one of me and TZ. Adorable. Oh—Flan, here's one of Alex. The girl in the picture with him is my oldest friend, Cookie Monsoon. She's really wild—*so* much fun. See?"

She shoved the phone under my nose. I squinted to make out the scene. There was Alex in his yellow Arden B. pin-striped shirt looking studly. He was sitting on a couch talking to some girl I didn't recognize. Huh. I leaned in for a better look. It was kind of blurry, but I could tell they were sitting really close.

Wait.

WAS ALEX KISSING HER?

Oh. My. God.

I could feel my knees go wobbly beneath me, and I stumbled back a little into SBB. She caught me around the waist, took the phone from my hands, and shoved it back at Kennedy.

"Oh, I'm sorry," Kennedy said innocently. "You probably didn't want to see that, did you?"

"What the hell is your problem, Kennedy?" SBB hissed.

Kennedy shrugged. "Look, maybe it's better that Flan know Alex is cheating on her. Imagine getting all the way to Paris only to be embarrassed in front of all your friends when he finally confesses."

I was reeling. The white restaurant was starting to look spotty and red, and I could tell I was going to faint if I didn't get out of there fast. Kennedy was still talking a mile a minute, but it was all starting to sound fuzzy in my ringing ears.

"We're getting out of here," SBB said, grabbing my hand.

It was the last thing I heard before everything went black.

$\mathcal{G}$et me smelling salts, mineral water, and a Gray's Papaya with relish. NO KETCHUP!"

A hazy voice was shouting orders somewhere over my head. I blinked. Where was I? I could feel myself moving, but I wasn't sure how. I tried to sit up, but a cool hand pressed down on my forehead.

"Shhh," the voice said. "Help is on the way."

Then, a whiff of the most pungent odor I had ever smelled infiltrated my nostrils. I wheezed and covered my face with my hands, coughing.

"And she's back," SBB said, smiling a very small and sad-looking smile at me. "Here's your revival cocktail." She handed me a bottle of sparkling Vittel water and a hot dog with a thick clump of relish down the middle, just the way I liked it.

"Where are we?" I asked, taking a bite.

"Getting you home," she said. "You really scared

me in there, Flannie. Luckily, Roderick was in the neighborhood and swung by Saks to pick us up." She pointed at the driver's seat of the Escalade that was speeding south down Fifth Avenue. That was when the awful truth came back to me. For the second time tonight, my stomach dropped down to my Derek Lam boots.

"Did I dream it?" I asked, trying to blot out the memory of that awful picture glaring in my brain.

"I don't think so, sweetie," SBB said. "But we're going to figure this out."

She was being so good to me, with her smooth hand stroking my forehead, but even though her words were confident, I could hear doubt in her voice. We'd both seen the evidence, clear as a Neutrogena model's skin. What was there to figure out?

"You have to talk to him," SBB said, as the car turned right on Houston Street. We drove past the Angelika theater, where Alex and I had gone to his friend's movie premiere party. We stopped at the light at Lafayette, in front of the twenty-four-hour pool hall where Alex recently taught me that there was more to the game than just the cool clicking noise the balls make when they knocked together.

No—I couldn't think about the good things at a

time like this. My mind spun back to last night, when I'd texted Alex because I had to back out of the party. He'd let me off the hook so easily. Now I wondered: had he already had Cookie Willderwhatsit waiting in the wings? The thought was too horrifying to bear.

SBB was right. Maybe there was a logical explanation behind all of this. Maybe Alex had a twin brother I didn't know about . . .

"It's going to be okay," I said, trying to convince myself with every word. "I just need to talk to him."

"That's right," SBB said, biting her lip. I had never seen her look so serious before. "The sooner you talk to that Jerk of New York—er, Alex, the better."

When the car turned west down Perry Street and came to a stop in front of my brownstone, I realized with a shock that I wasn't going to have to wait very long. Alex was sitting on my front steps. He looked like he'd been there a while.

I whipped around to face SBB, my eyes wide.

"Do I look okay?" I asked. I couldn't believe the words even escaped my lips. Alex knew me so well, he didn't care if I just rolled out of bed or if I was walking down a runway. But suddenly, I felt pressure to look my best.

SBB pinched my cheeks. "There," she said. "Now you've got your color back. You look great." She held my hand. "Flan," she said, looking deep in my eyes.

I nodded. "Don't let him off the hook too easily. I know you care about him, but—"

I nodded again and started to open the door of the car.

"Flan," she whispered loudly. "Do you want to take the smelling salts? Just in case?"

I forced a smile. "No thanks," I said. "Hopefully I've maxed out my blackout potential for one night. I'll call you later?"

SBB held up both her hands with her pointer and middle fingers crossed, our secret sign for good luck. I returned the gesture, and with that, slid down from the car and went to face Alex on the steps.

He was wearing his Diesel jeans with the rip in the thigh from when we'd hopped that fence to get into the Knicks game a few weeks ago. His dark hair was still damp, probably from the shower he'd taken after lacrosse practice. He smelled so good, like pine needles and—no. I couldn't get all swoony again. I needed my wits about me.

"Hi," I said stiffly.

"Hi," he said. He didn't stand up to kiss me, like he always did, so I just took a seat next to him. But just as I was sitting down, he started to stand up and moved in for a kiss, which missed my lips and landed awkwardly on my nose.

Normally, we would have cracked up about that. But neither one of us seemed to think it was funny tonight.

"How are you?" he asked.

"Good."

"What's wrong?"

"Nothing," I said quickly. "What's wrong with you?"

"Nothing."

"Oh."

There was a weird pause, and then Alex asked, "Excited about Paris?"

"Uh-huh," I said, not looking at him. "Are you?"

Out of the corner of my eye, I could see him nod. We stared out at the empty street and watched a pigeon waddle by. This was awful—and so not *us*.

Finally, Alex turned to me.

"Look, Flan, there's something I think we should talk about."

Oh my God, oh my God. He was going to bring it up. He was going to tell me that he'd fallen in love with a girl named *Cookie*, and that he was spending spring break with her on a deserted island, and that both of them were Team Kennedy now. I was so mortified and so hurt. I knew right then that I couldn't even stand to hear his explanation.

"I have something I need to say too," I said quickly.

"You do?" he asked, eyebrows raised.

"I know what happened last night," I said.

"*You do?*" he said, sounding shocked. "And?"

"And I'm appalled," I said. "I thought things were going so well with us."

"Me too," he said. "But then—"

"I don't want to hear it," I said briskly, cutting him off. I was surprised that I was on such a roll. Usually I'd have crumbled by now, but I just held my ground and said, "I think Kennedy already told me everything I needed to know."

"So you and Kennedy have already talked about it," he said. He sounded disappointed. "I wanted to be the first—"

"Too late," I huffed. "Kennedy's not exactly the person I wanted to hear it from either. But when she showed me that picture—"

"Picture?" Alex asked.

At the mention of the picture of Alex and—shudder—*Cookie*, I felt my throat start to constrict. I was *not* going to cry. If I cried, he would put his arms around me—or worse—he wouldn't. Either way, I couldn't handle it. I needed to stay strong.

"I don't want to get into it," I said. "I'm sure you understand."

Alex looked confused, but nodded. "So what do we do?" he asked.

"You haven't left us with much choice," I sniffed. "Obviously we have to break up. I can't be with someone who's not committed."

"What? No. We don't have to break up."

I couldn't believe he was going to cheat on me and then argue for us to stay together. That was just plain insulting.

"Are you kidding? I can barely stand to look at you right now. I can't be your girlfriend after this—much less go to Paris with you."

Alex's mouth dropped open. He shook his head. Then he stood up and started pacing the sidewalk. "I can't believe this. All because of one little—"

"Believe it," I said.

"So it's over?" he asked. I could have sworn his eyes looked moist. "Just like that?"

This was my chance—to make him grovel and apologize and swear I was the only girl for him. But deep in my heart, I knew, I'd never be able to get that picture out of my head. And I'd never forgive Alex for acting like this wasn't such a big deal. I looked at his tortured face in front of me. I did get a little bit of solace that at least he looked half as broken up as I felt inside. I was about to do the hardest thing I'd ever done in my life. I took a deep breath and met his eyes.

"It's over," I said. "Just like that."

$\mathcal{T}$he girls and I had agreed to meet at Candle Café for breakfast before school on Friday. Originally, the plan had been to go over the final details before the red-eye flight that night. But since my whole world had come crashing down on me twelve hours ago, things were looking slightly different. When my Betty Boop alarm clock went off at six-thirty, I groaned, rolled over, and buried my face in my pillow. The sound was so unwelcome, I wanted to throw Betty against the wall.

Noodles, the world's greatest Pomeranian, chose that moment to pounce on my neck and start attacking me with kisses. He could always sense when I need a little extra love. This morning, I was so utterly devastated—I needed a whole lot of extra love.

It wasn't going to be easy to break the news to my friends. For starters, breaking the news meant I was going to have to relive every excruciating detail—starting with Kennedy's sneer at Saks and ending with the sight of Alex, walking away down Perry Street without even looking back. Then I was going to have to tell them that my eyes were already too red from crying to take the red-eye. I had to tell them I was going be a GPA no-show.

All of this was made even worse by the fact that everyone was depending on me to be the ringleader. Just thinking about all my friends right now—innocently blow-drying their hair at home (Harper), accidentally oversleeping (Camille), illegally downloading one more song for our trip's mix CDs (Morgan), and making a last-minute decision to throw both pairs of hot pink jeans in her suitcase (Amory)—made me panic. None of them had a clue that I was about to drop the biggest bomb, possibly in the history of spring break.

We'd decided to meet at Candle Café because a) it was super healthy and super delicious (one last cleansing day before we consumed half the butter in Paris) and b) because it was our last day to dine somewhere that was *so* Manhattan. As Camille pointed out, there was little chance we'd be eating macrobiotic quinoa in Paris.

But there was just one problem: the vegan chefs at

Candle swore by that very special (read: imposter!) food product called carob. The dessert list was all carob puddings and carob chip soy ice cream, etc. And everybody knows that there are times in life when a girl needs the real thing.

Today was a chocolate day if I'd ever seen one.

To help arm myself for the difficult conversation I knew I had ahead of me, I swung by the nearby Crumbs en route to Candle Café. I'd always wondered why a cupcake shop needed to open at seven in the morning—but today I understood. When I saw the shaven-headed, nose-ringed, white-aproned baker slide a tray of luscious-looking cupcakes into the glass case before me, I knew she was going to be my savior.

"Can I have that double chocolate cupcake—no, to the left . . . the big one?" I pointed to the case and waited for the biggest, swirliest, chocolatiest cupcake in all of Crumbs to be delivered to me in a little paper bag.

"There's nothing these cupcakes can't fix, is there?" she asked, ringing me up.

I was afraid that if I opened my mouth to disagree, I would start to cry. Either that or delve into way too much personal information. So I just nodded, tried to smile, and dashed out the door with my cupcake. I was already five minutes late for breakfast, and I could feel the GPA binder burning in my Jamin Puech patched leather Sheriffa bag.

Candle Café was already packed with power-breakfasting Upper East Siders, but I quickly spotted my friends huddled together at the back of the restaurant. I sidled past the hissing espresso machine and sank into the one remaining empty chair, thumping my cupcake on the table.

Camille eyed the paper bag, saw the big Crumbs logo, and raised her eyebrows at me. "You do know that they serve food here, too?" she joked. Her eyes widened when she watched me pull the massive cupcake out of the bag and take a gigantic bite.

"Oh my God," Morgan said. "That looks so freaking good. I wonder if I can cancel my oatmeal—wait, Flan, why are you eating half a pound of chocolate before eight a.m.?"

"Let's just say it's one of those days," I said, keeping my mouth full so I wouldn't have to talk much more. I could already feel the tears welling up, and I knew the girls would be onto me instantly.

Amory put her hand on my arm. "Uh-oh. What's going on, babe?" she asked. "Talk to us."

I wanted to start at the beginning, to try to make sense out of what was still so baffling to me, but when I opened my mouth, what came out was a small mournful wail, a few crumbs of cupcake, and "Icaaaaan'tgotoPaaaaaris."

"What?" all five of them said at once.

"What happened?"

"Don't even joke about that!"

"Are you crazy?"

I hiccuped and blew my nose on my napkin.

"It's Alex," I sniffed, shaking my head. "It's too awful to tell."

"Worse than when Xander accidentally shaved off his eyebrows?" Camille joked. But when she saw the dire expression on my face, her smile disappeared.

"Alex cheated on me," I said, looking down at the remains of my cupcake.

A collective gasp that was heard around the restaurant escaped my friends' lips. Before I knew it, all four of their hands were holding mine and the whole story came pouring out, along with more than a few tears.

"The nerve," Harper huffed, showing a rare burst of temper.

"And you had to hear about it from Kennedy," Amory said, making all five of us shudder. "What's worse?"

"What's worse is Flan saying she's not coming to Paris," Camille said. She started tugging on her hair, hard, like she did when she was really nervous.

"Well, we'll stay in the city with you," Morgan said decidedly. "We'll have another boy boycott."

"No," I said. "No way. No more boy boycotts. You have to go to Paris. Someone should enjoy it."

My friends nodded halfheartedly, but I could see them looking nervously back and forth at each other. It was kind of like we were mourning the death of the GPA—and I really didn't want that to happen. Still, I couldn't exactly hold the position of trip advisor remotely. If I didn't go to Paris, what would happen to all our plans?

"Does, uh, does anyone else speak French?" Amory said.

Her question was met by blank stares across the table.

"Maybe one of the boys does?" Morgan offered. "Sometimes Bennett does this really cute French accent when we go to cafés. . . ." She trailed off.

"We don't even know where we're staying," Harper realized.

"Or how to take the Métro," Amory added.

"Or the address of Jade Moodswing's atelier," Camille agreed.

The girls were getting totally freaked out. There was only one thing to do.

For the very last time, I pulled the GPA binder out

of my bag and laid it on the table. "I'm officially turning this over to you guys now. Everything you need to know is in here. Restaurant reservations, shopping routes, Jade's cell phone," I said gravely. "Treat it well."

The girls looked at the binder in the middle of the table like it was some sort of oracle. Finally, Camille reached for it and placed it on her lap.

"It's in good hands," she said, stroking its glossy top cover. "But I still hate the thought of you not being with us."

"You understand though, right?" I asked.

The girls nodded. "What are you going to do about Alex?" Camille asked.

"Honestly," I said, "I have no idea. How am I supposed to get over this?"

I looked at my friends, who looked at each other. We'd all definitely had our share of boy drama, but no one had really had boy *trauma* of this caliber yet. Full-fledged cheating was uncharted territory among our clique.

"You're really brave, Flan," Amory said, sipping the last of her double espresso.

"And if Alex doesn't see that . . ." Harper agreed, popping a strawberry in her mouth.

"He doesn't deserve you," Morgan finished, signaling the waiter for the check.

"You'll call us every day?" Camille said. "Three times a day at least?"

"And vice versa," I said, trying to sound brave. But when I tried to imagine answering the phone to hear about what the girls had gotten from Jade's atelier, or how they liked the Eiffel Tower, all I could see was my sad self lying at home on the couch with bad takeout food, a box of tissues, Noodles, and a slew of Netflix DVDs. Your basic recipe for disaster. I had to come up with a better plan.

What was I going to do over spring break?

*M*oping along the sidewalk on my way home from school, the direness of my situation finally started to sink in. I had just called it quits on the most important relationship in my life—in a really mortifying, every-girl's-worst-nightmare kind of way—and what was worse, practically everyone I knew was fleeing the city and leaving me all alone to wallow.

All alone. I could almost hear the tearjerker sound track picking up behind me as I shuffled down Perry Street.

"Flan?"

My head jerked up.

"What are you doing here—all alone?"

The voice came from a limousine, which pulled to a stop in front of me and rolled down its window. When I saw the big black D&G shades, I breathed a sigh of relief. It was my mom.

"Aren't you supposed to be on your way to the airport, with your friends? Flan—have you been crying?"

Before I could open my mouth, the door of the limo opened up and my mother practically swooped me into the seat next to her. I collapsed on the plush black leather armrest and buried my face in her red cashmere pashmina.

"It's never good to cry on the street," my mom said. Then she grinned the way she did when she thought she was having an especially good idea. "Especially when you have a mother with a four o'clock Swedish massage appointment at Spa Bloomie's. Hold on, I'll squeeze you in."

Some people are good at playing piano, others have a green thumb for gardening. My mother was born with the insurmountable gift of being able to get any reservation for anything, anywhere, in under thirty seconds. She made a call, and I was in at Spa Bloomie's for a four o'clock with Helga.

Well, at least when my friends were sharing all their fabulous Paris stories, I'd have one thing to tell them I did over spring break.

"Okay," Mom said as we drove south on Broadway. "Spill it."

By the time we got to Bloomingdale's, my mom

knew all the gory Alex details, and she'd given me a week's worth of full-body hugs (I stopped counting at about thirteen). Mom was always great to talk to, but tonight she was being especially supportive.

"I didn't know I could cry this much," I said, wincing when I caught a glimpse of my mascara-streaked face in the mirror above the icebox.

"You're a woman. Women are tear factories," my mom said. "The good news is you're also a Flood, which is how I know you're going to get through this. Men will come and go, you know that. But a Flood will—"

"I know, I know: a Flood will never crash." It was what my parents had been telling us our whole lives—whenever Patch failed an exam at Princeton, or when one of Feb's movies didn't get funded—all of life's little upsets were met with the very same mantra. Sometimes it made me feel better to know that I came from a family with such strength, but today, it made my stomach hurt. It felt like too little, too late. Did I have to tell my mom that this Flood might have already crashed at the first mention of the word *Cookie*?

As my mom and I walked into Bloomingdale's toward the spa upstairs, I couldn't stop looking at all the new spring clothes and beach-themed displays set up to woo shoppers on their way to sunny locales. It was yet another reminder that my spring break was going to completely suck.

"What's with the face?" my mom asked, steering me into the calming back room of the spa. "Did you want the hot stone instead of the Swedish?"

"No, I love the Swedish. It's just that . . . well," I stammered. "All my friends are leaving for Paris tonight. I guess I'm just practicing my solo-wallowing face for the rest of spring break."

My mom shot me a look like I was crazy. "Nonsense," she said. "You'll come to the Amalfi Coast with your father and me. It'll be just the thing." She nodded once before stepping into the dressing room to change into her white terry cloth robe. Her tone suggested that there was no question that a trip to Italy was exactly what I needed.

"Really?" I brightened. I reached for my own robe and slipped out of my TwillTwentyTwo cargo pants in the dressing room next to my mom. "I wouldn't be in the way?"

"Darling, don't make me beg," my mom joked. "Your father wants to go cheese tasting, of all things. I'll need a companion for scoping out those dark-haired Italian stallions. Of course, we'll just look. And of course you're coming. I'll make a call. Can you be ready to leave tonight?"

"I'm a Flood," I said, using my mom's favorite phrase.

We both came out of the dressing room at the same time and she gave me my umpteenth hug of the afternoon. "Good," she said. "Now enjoy your massage and we'll talk packing strategies once we're both refreshed."

I stepped into the dimly lit massage room, my spirits partially lifted. I hung my robe on the door and climbed onto the cool padded massage mat, pulling the terry cloth blanket over me. The Bloomingdale's spa always carried the store's best soy candles, so the whole room smelled like vanilla and pomegranate. I had almost fallen into a restful sleep, when I felt some very therapeutic hands on my shoulders.

"I'm Helga," the masseuse said soothingly. "I am here to take care of your every need. What concerns you this afternoon?"

"Well," I said, surprising myself by opening up to the masseuse, "I do have a bit of a broken heart."

"Mmm." I could feel her nodding over me. "Then I'll give you the 'scorned lover.' In eleven years of practicing, it's never failed."

As Helga went to work on my upper shoulders and neck, I could feel myself relaxing. Despite my negative outlook, it was actually one of the best Swedish massages I'd ever had. I guess plummeting to the depths of despair really makes you appreciate the little things in life.

I was still obviously a wreck about Alex, but at least now I had these super-relaxed shoulder muscles. And my parents to keep me sane this week. And an upcoming new stamp on my passport. In fact, I was feeling so much better that halfway through my massage, I found myself wanting to call my Thoney friends to tell them about my revised schedule. But then, I knew they'd all be rushing to get their gear together for the flight tonight.

Ooh, I knew who I could call. But would that be weird in the middle of Helga's heart-healing massage? I dared to peek my head back and saw her smiling blond head looking down at me.

"Helga?" I asked. "Would you mind if I called my friend while you worked? It's about my ex, and I just think it would really help."

"Are you kidding, honey? If they let me talk to my shrink while I worked, I'd never hang up. Be my guest."

Sweet. I scooted forward on the bed to reach for my cell phone. Helga kept up the good work and I dialed SBB.

"So, did you try the voodoo yet?" her voice chirped when she picked up.

"Voodoo?" I asked. "Huh?"

"I e-mailed you about it this morning. You know, you order one of those dolls online, paste a picture of Jony's face where the head is, and throw pins at it? I haven't tried it, but my friend said—"

"I might hold off on the voodoo for at least a few more days," I said. "Wait, who's Jony?"

"The Jerk of New York," SBB said. "We need to start calling him that. How do you expect to get over him if you don't take desperate measures?"

"That's what I'm calling to tell you," I said. "My parents are taking me to the Amalfi Coast in southern Italy for the week. My dad's scoping out some cheese, and my mom's scoping out some Italian men—anyway, we're leaving tonight."

"Oh my God!" SBB shrieked over the phone, making Helga jump a little. "I love Capri! It's just off the coast. You must go there! Did I ever tell you how once I rented a moped with my costar of *Amalfi Amour*—you remember Don Garrett? Obviously, he was *way* too old for me, *kinda* wrinkly, but boy, could he take curves at high speeds!"

I coughed into the phone.

"Sorry," SBB said. "You were saying?"

"I was saying," I explained, "that I think it will be good for me to get some space from New York, from all the Alex—er, Jony memories. Plus my parents always lighten me up. They won't let me act all mopey and depressing—"

"As is your wont," SBB said.

"Hey!" I said defensively, feeling Helga's hands smooth out my shoulders.

"Come on, Flan, I know you. Until your mom suggested you join them in Italy for spring break—probably at some spa . . . Are you at Bliss?"

"Bloomingdale's," I admitted with a laugh.

"Uh-huh," she said. "That was my next guess. Anyway, until your mom suggested it, you were totally planning on sitting home alone, getting Noodles's perfect fur all frizzy with your tears. Am I right?"

"Well . . ." I sighed. "Sorta."

"Am I good or am I good?" SBB laughed. "Just be glad you're going to Italy. I was this close to hiring Bianca to assist you in your time of need."

"Wait," I said. "Who's Bianca?"

"Oh, just this Serbian wonder woman I know. Some call her a witch—but I prefer not to categorize people. She's got a patented technique for heartbreak. Basically, she takes a sob story, mulls it over, and eradicates all feelings of residual love. She's a genius."

I wasn't sure about the use of the word *eradicate*

when it came to emotional loss, but I didn't think now was the time to argue.

"I won't scare you with the details—maybe I'll just send you the link to her website. Then again, maybe the sunshine, the gelato, and perhaps an Italian *fling* will be enough for your broken heart?"

"Sigh," I said. "I'm not really there yet, but I guess I'm going to give Italy my best shot."

"Oh, Flannie, I wish I could go with you," she said wistfully.

"Please! I would love to have the SBB-guided tour of the Amalfi Coast. I can't guarantee I'm brave enough to cart you around on a moped, but . . . please come!" I pleaded.

SBB sighed. "If only I weren't committed to being in L.A. all week. I'm reading lines for *Gladiatrix* and I'm totally freaking out about it. I've only gained two pounds of muscle this week." She paused. "Tell you what: if you come back from Italy and you're totally over Jony—and in the meantime, I get the part—I will throw us both a huge We Rule celebration. Anywhere you want."

Behind me, Helga tapped my shoulder lightly.

"We're finished here, Flan. I'll let you get dressed. I hope everything works out for you, romantically and otherwise."

I mouthed thanks to Helga as I mulled over SBB's offer. It was certainly tempting, and I did really want SBB to get the part. But from my mental state, being "totally" over Alex—well, it seemed so far away.

I had to ask: "What if I'm not over Jony?"

"Well then," SBB said seriously, "we'll have to resort to Bianca, won't we? That's not a promise—it's a threat. Now get to Italy and get over him, okay?"

*B*uongiorno, bella," a trim, dark-haired flight attendant whispered softly in my ear the next morning. "We'll be landing in Naples in half an hour. Can I get you some espresso? A breakfast panini? Gelato?"

I glanced down at my watch. It was barely past midnight New York time, but I could already see the sun peeking through windows of the eight-seater private jet my parents had chartered to take us to Naples. I blinked up at the handsome flight attendant, whose name tag read LUIGI. Even though I hardly ever passed up the opportunity to indulge in a little gelato, I hadn't been able to stomach much since the breakup.

"An espresso sounds great," I told Luigi, who winked and whisked himself off to the kitchen, giving me quite a view of the back of his fitted white trousers. Who knew my parents traveled with such attractive hospitality?

"Isn't he *fabulous*?" My mom leaned across the aisle. She had her sleep mask perched on her forehead. I looked over at the window seat next to her, where my dad's own mask was still firmly in place over his eyes.

"Of course, your father is my one and only," my mom continued. "But when he put me in charge of staffing the jet, I figured it couldn't hurt to hire eye candy, as long as they got the job done. You know what they say—a woman can never be too rich, too skinny, or surrounded by too many gorgeous men."

"Did somebody say gorgeous men?" my dad asked sleepily, pulling up his eye mask and the window shade. "Look no further, ladies."

My mom leaned over to kiss him, and an unexpected pang of sadness shot through me. I'd seen my parents kiss a million times, but never on the heels of such an earth-shattering breakup.

I was relieved when Luigi returned with espressos for all of us, and super excited when he also brought these incredibly buttery Italian cookies that were phenomenal dipped in the coffee. Maybe I did have my appetite back. I focused my attention on drowning my sorrows in sugar, caffeine, and the ridiculously beautiful views outside as the plane came into Naples.

From the moment we touched down, I could feel the energy of Italy. We were only at the airport, but I sort of have a sixth sense about these things. Out the window, I could see the ground crew shouting orders at each other with a ferocity that reminded me a little of New York, but mixed with a cool European vibe.

When we deplaned and followed the ramp toward customs, there was a definite bustle in the airport around us. Noisy tourists shoved past each other, and everyone was shouting in different languages. But somehow, there seemed to be a shield between my family and all the other noise. Nothing fazed us. We marched straight through customs, and our bags were waiting for us in the town car parked outside. Less than twenty minutes after landing, we were on our way to the private ferry that would take us down to the Amalfi Coast.

I checked my watch again. It was a goal of mine to stop being obsessed with what time it was in New York, but so far, I hadn't made much progress. It was nine in the morning Naples time, which meant it was three a.m. in New York. I hoped Alex was tossing and turning miserably in his bed. Either that or having nightmares about what a huge mistake he'd made by cheating on me . . . Hold on. I could *not* spend a whole week thinking about what Alex was up to every second of the day.

Better to think about my friends in Paris. I tried to imagine them—would they be enjoying croissants and cappuccinos along the Seine by now? No, they'd only landed an hour ago. They were probably still stuck at baggage claim at Charles de Gaulle, where my online research had told me that the ground crew went on strike at least three times a week. I knew I should have told Camille to expect delays at the airport when I handed over the GPA binder. Would they be able to manage without me?

I pulled out my phone and sent a hurried text to make sure that everything was going okay so far.

"Flan." My mother's voice interrupted me from across the town car. "Why the furrowed brow? You're in Italy, if you hadn't noticed."

As usual, Mom was right. With the kids on bikes, tiny cars, and teens on scooters, it was hard not to notice that we were in Italy as we zoomed through the crazy streets of Naples. And I thought New York taxi drivers were insane. But even with the blaring horns of nearby cars ringing in my ears, the ease of traveling with my parents was soothing.

"Here we are," my dad said as we pulled into a small marina. "Right on time—and of course, there's Alfonso with the *Duchess*." He gestured to a gleaming white yacht at the end of a marina. "It's a beautiful boat, Flan. You'll love the captain, too; he tells the best stories about his days in the Navy—"

"Richard, do you want to bore your own daughter to death?" my mom interrupted. "Flan, trust me, do not ask Alfonso about the war. You just sit back, relax, and enjoy the sea breeze on your youthful skin, okay?"

"Sounds good to me." I laughed.

I followed my parents down the dock toward the *Duchess*. She was an eighteen-foot yacht with a large, pristine deck, and sails that extended way up into the sunny sky. Somehow, the town car driver hauled all three of our bags over his shoulders, and even lifted my carry-on bag in the crook of his arm. There was someone to do everything for us here.

"Special delivery," a good-looking guy about my age said with a grin. "I know you love our margherita, Signore Flood." He had dark hair, dimples—and the biggest box of pizza I had ever seen, balanced on his shoulder.

My dad shrugged at me. "I always have one of Tony's famous pizzas delivered to the docks when we land. It just starts the trip off right. Here," he said, taking the box from the delivery boy. "It's my daughter's first time in Italy—she should have the first bite."

"You know what they say." the boy grinned. "One bite of Tony's mozzarella and an American girl cannot help but fall in love."

With both my parents, the chauffeur, Alfonso the yacht captain, and the more-and-more-gorgeous-with-every-accented-word-he-said delivery boy all watching me, I nervously opened the box of pizza, picked up a wide floppy slice, and took a bite.

Ohhhmygod. You grow up in the city and think you know a thing or two about good pizza. Then you go to Italy and your mind gets absolutely blown.

"You're right," I said to the delivery boy, my mouth still full of hot tomato sauce and cheese. "I think I am in love."

"Sweetheart," my dad said, putting his arm around me, "there's more where that came from. Hop on the *Duchess* and we'll see how many times you fall in love this week."

With those auspicious words, we waved good-bye to the pizza boy and the driver, and spread out on the top deck of the yacht. Alfonso came by to kiss both of my parents on both cheeks. When he was introduced to me, he wrapped me in his arms and kept saying the word *bellissima*.

"Italian men have a soft spot for blondes," my mom explained, shaking her head. "I'm afraid you're going to get quite a lot of attention this week."

It was kind of unexpected to have strangers kissing me and showering me with compliments, but then again, in light of the Jony saga, maybe attention from strangers was exactly what I needed.

A few minutes after Alfonso steered the yacht out of the Naples marina, he came by with a tray of sparkling water, olives, and a bowl of sliced citrus fruit, marinated in this sweet, tangy syrup.

"Sweet, sparkly, and a little bit salty," he explained with a twinkling grin. "Just like we hope your trip will be in Italy."

The trip from Naples to Sorrento, the small coastal town where we were staying, took about forty-five minutes. My parents and I found spots to recline on the soft seats of the deck and closed our eyes. I could feel the warm sun beating down on us, but a cool ocean breeze kept it comfortable. And little by little, the noise from the marina was replaced with the lapping sounds of the sparkling Mediterranean.

Before I knew it, we were docking again. When I opened my eyes this time, the view of Sorrento took my breath away. There were high stone walls leading up to the city, and orange trees in full bloom dotting almost every part of the coast. I could see umbrellas set up all along the waterfront and tables full of very stylish patrons enjoying a leisurely lunch.

"I knew you'd love it here," my dad said, grinning at my excited expression. "Just wait until you take a spin through town."

A crew arrived to transport our bags up the high stairs to where the large, private villa my parents had bought last year stood at the edge of the coastline. They'd been here several times since then, and I'd seen more than a few slide shows of photos from their travels, but nothing prepared me for the view when my parents opened up the French doors to the room where I'd be staying.

"Do you think you can manage here for a week?" my mother asked, suddenly sounding nervous. "I hope it's not too drafty. If we'd known you were coming sooner, I would have had them install another sky-light, but—"

"It's perfect," I breathed.

The cool stone tiles were the same golden color as the sun, which was now high in the sky. The bed faced the balcony, which looked out at the sea, which seemed to go on forever. From here, New York felt so far away—and for the first time since we'd left the city, I was glad.

"We thought we'd have a relaxing day after all the hectic travel," my mom said. She seemed unaware of the fact that, compared to most people's experience, our day of travel had been anything but hectic. "Dad's going to order dinner from the café down the street. We'll take it out on the balcony and chill. Sound good?"

I sort of loved to hate my mom's tendency to use lingo a generation below hers, but I was happy to hear the word *chill*.

"It sounds great." I laughed.

We each claimed a plush chaise lounge on the main balcony and basked in the fantastic Amalfi sun. Even though we'd just chowed down on Tony's famous margarita pizza, I somehow found room for about six more courses that my dad insisted I try before going to sleep. Each one was better than the one before it.

"Why didn't anyone ever tell me about spumoni before?" I gasped, spooning up the pistachio, chocolate, and strawberry ice creamy deliciousness in my bowl. "This stuff is definitely going on my list of 'things to be eaten again ASAP.'"

"That's my daughter." My dad beamed.

I could see my parents sharing relieved looks that I

was a) getting nourishment and b) occasionally smiling. Usually I prided myself on the fact that I was self-sufficient, but today it felt good to be taken care of.

On the glass table next to me, I saw my cell phone buzz. I practically leapt to pick it up. It was a text from Camille. I hadn't heard from her all day.

YOU'LL NEVER BELIEVE IT—WE JUST LEFT CHARLES DE GAULLE. ALL THE BAGGAGE HANDLERS WERE ON STRIKE ALL DAY! YOU WOULD HAVE DIED. BUT IT WAS HILARIOUS BECAUSE ONE OF THEM FELL IN LOOOOVE WITH AMORY, AND HE TOOK HER TO THE BACK ROOM TO LOOK FOR HER STUFF. JASON GOT ADORABLY JEALOUS. BUT NEVER MIND OUR BORING DETAILS—HOW ARE YOU?

Crazy. My biggest organization fear for the trip had come true. My friends had spent the whole day at the airport, which meant they'd missed their reservations at the Louvre and probably hadn't even gotten into the city in time to eat dinner at Sud on rue Cler.

But strangely, Camille's text made it sound like it had actually been sort of an adventure. Oh, I wanted to be there so badly!

I looked over at my parents, who were both serenely enjoying the scenery, and I remembered that my purpose this week was different from my friends'. I was taking care of Flan.

Here I was on this gorgeous balcony, eating amazing

food, with the world's most supersupportive parents. Things were going to be okay. Before I knew it, I felt myself drifting off to sleep. The cool Amalfi breeze was in my hair, and I wasn't even thinking about what time it was in New York.

9:55 A.M., SUNDAY MORNING
Standing outside Sorrento's motorcycle
rental shop:

How incredible is Italy? You don't even have to be a licensed driver to rent a scooter. Which puts fourteen-year-old me in very good standing for some serious coastal cruising. Get yer motor running!

10:02 A.M., SUNDAY MORNING
One block . . . and two small fender
benders later:

What is wrong with this country? Don't they have laws? Why would anyone rent a scooter to a teenage Manhattanite who's never been behind the wheel of anything in her life?

"Flan! Are you okay?" my mom gasped. She

flipped up the plastic eye shield on her helmet, hopped off her own bike, and started running toward me—and the second unlucky lamppost I'd just hit. "Thank God you were wearing your helmet!"

"Oh, that's what fenders are for," my dad said casually, hopping off his bike to survey the scene. We were just outside the cobblestone streets of downtown Sorrento, on a main road connecting all the small towns along the coast. We had been on our way to visit a small waterfront cathedral—until my bad driving brought that plan to a screeching halt.

"Just a small scratch on the lamppost," my dad said. "And no damage to the bike, luckily. You're not hurt, are you, sweetheart?"

"Just a little shaken up," I said, attempting to take off my helmet and realizing that I was actually a lot shaken up. "I'll never make fun of Feb again for getting so many reckless-driving tickets. I had no idea it was so hard."

I felt my mom's arms envelop me. "Darling, I think you just have a lot on your mind. Why not ride on the back of your father's bike and just take in the sights?"

I nodded and sighed. Riding my own bike around the curving coastline had seemed like such a good idea at the time—it was the kind of thing that would make a really great story to tell my friends, anyway.

But it was actually a lot scarier than it looked. I took one last look at my enemy—the lamppost—and decided I'd be much happier riding tandem with my dad.

After a quick exchange at the bike shop, we were down to two scooters, speeding out toward the shrine. I held on tight to my dad, feeling much more secure taking those hairpin turns. This was more like it!

I'd woken up this morning to a surprise from my parents: breakfast in bed—a brimming bowl of strawberries; warm, crusty ciabatta and fresh butter; a pot of that fantastic Italian coffee—*and* the very good news that both of them were putting aside their business matters for the whole day. According to Dad, Mom's vacation-only mandate had gone out the window when Nicoletta Dimore offered her a guest blogging spot reviewing a spa for her online zine.

All morning, my parents had been jokingly referring to today as "Flan gets cultured," which I only objected to slightly. I went to museums in the city! Sometimes. But my parents were clearly pretty serious about making the most of our day together. They'd really crammed in the sightseeing, starting with the ride out to this historic cathedral on the coast, moving right along to a boat cruise to the island of Capri, where we were going cheese tasting and shopping. Mom insisted that the stores in Capri gave Fifth Avenue a run for its money.

I loved having my parents all to myself—and against such a beautiful backdrop, too. Looking around at the steep cliffs dropping down to all that crazy blue water, it was hard to believe that people actually lived here and got to see these views every day. But then again, I knew people said that about Manhattan all the time. Crap—I wasn't supposed to be thinking about Manhattan. It only led to me thinking about—

"Flan," my dad said. "We're here."

Happy to be snapped out of my downward-spiraling thoughts, I hopped off the bike and joined my parents at the door of the cathedral. The hush inside the church was almost a shock to my system after spending so long listening to the roar of the bike, but once I stepped inside, I understood why every-thing was so quiet.

The stained glass windows and old stone pews were so beautiful, they demanded a silent sort of rev-erence. I separated from my parents and walked through the church on my own, reading what signs I could find in English. It was actually really fun to try to make out some of the Italian using what I knew from French. When I came to the end of the dimly lit church, I pushed open the back door and was almost startled by the intense sunlight flooding into the backyard. It was a small, irregularly shaped plot of grass at the tip of a crag on the cliff. A low stone fence was the only thing separating me from the drop-off into the sea. I had never seen anything so magnificent— and I'd been to a lot of fashion shows.

"Flan," my father's voice whispered. "You have to see this Michelangelo." He led me around to the side of the church, where a large marble sculpture was prominently positioned so that it absolutely glowed in the sun. I could tell it was a man's body, but half of the marble looked like it was still uncut, just the natural shape of the stone.

"Why does it look like that?" I asked my dad. "Is it unfinished?"

He shook his head. "A lot of Michelanglo's work looks like this. People say he thought his job was to release the essence of the figure inside."

I walked in a full circle around the sculpture. It was fascinating and beautiful, but there was also something disappointing about only halfway releasing the sculpture from the stone. It was like you could see all this amazing potential cut short. Kind of like a certain relationship I knew. Ugh.

"I think I'm ready for the next stop on the 'Flan gets cultured' tour," I said quickly.

We climbed back on the scooters and my dad zig-zagged his way down to the water, where the *Duchess* was waiting for us. Alfonso stepped forward to kiss us again, and we reclaimed our seats on the deck. The ride out to Capri was even more relaxing than yesterday's ride from Naples had been. The sea was calm and clear, and there were only a few other boats in view. In the distance, Capri rose up like a volcano in the middle of a vast flat line of blue water.

"This is a magical island," Alfonso said, steering the boat toward Capri. "With caves as blue as your eyes and limoncello as sweet as your smile."

My mom looked at me and rolled her eyes at the cheesiness, but surprisingly, I was sort of into it. Italian people just told you when they liked you—they never lied to you or cheated on you with girls named Cookie, or—uh-oh. Zip it, Flan.

When we docked at the small marina in Capri, I followed my parents to a funicular that took us all the way up the mountain in under two minutes. It was impossible to let your eyes fall somewhere that didn't look like a postcard.

"Marco's cheese shop is just over this way," my dad said when we climbed out of the funicular. "Brace yourself, Flan, okay?"

Out of everyone in my family, my dad and I are the

biggest foodies. I can't count the number of times we've bored my mom and siblings making them do a taste test to pick their favorite goat cheese from Murray's down the block. Mom always indulged us, at least for a little while, and I could tell today that she'd struck a compromise with my dad: cheese tasting first for him, followed by shopping for her. Lucky for me, I loved both.

"What are you sampling today, Marco?" my dad asked a heavy mustached man when the three of us entered the tiny side-street shop. "I brought my daughter all the way from New York City and told her you're the best."

Marco's face lit up at the sight of me. "Oh," he said, "for such a *bella ragazza*, I must go back to my storeroom for something super special!"

I blushed at the compliment and Marco shuffled off to the back, returning moments later with a tray full of unfamiliar cheeses. Following my dad's lead, I sampled this really sharp Gorgonzola, aged pecorino with peppercorns, and hands down the best burrata on the planet.

"Ooh." Marco grinned when I reached for a second piece of the melt-in-your-mouth buffalo mozzarella. "She likes that one, I can tell. I have one more very special one, very rare. Only for you to taste today."

He reached under the counter and pulled out a small parcel wrapped in brown paper. When he unwrapped it, all three of us caught a pungent whiff and jumped back.

"Strong, eh?" Marco laughed, holding out a few crumbled pieces in his palm. "Aged pecorino. You'll love it! Don't be scared."

It wasn't that I was scared of the cheese—it was just that the odor reminded me of something . . . sort of like smelly gym socks . . . but no, that wasn't exactly it. At the prompting of my parents, I reached for the smallest piece of the cheese and hesitantly popped it in my mouth.

There it was: this cheese had the exact same smell as Alex's gym bag did after a lacrosse tournament. I was eating my cheating ex-boyfriend's sweaty gym bag. Could it get any lower than this?

Marco's face fell. "She hates it," he murmured.

"No!" I insisted, making myself swallow the lump of cheese. "It's wonderful. Very unique. I just . . . I was thinking about something else."

"She was thinking about shopping, maybe," my mom prompted, tapping her watch. "About how maybe Flan would like to see another side of Capri before all the stores close? Hint, hint."

I nodded my agreement, and after my father

bought half the cheese in Marco's shop, we stepped back out to the street, ready to hit the stores.

Mom was right about the shopping scene in Capri. For such a tiny little island, they had a lot of big-name designers lining the streets. One stop into Louis Vuitton, Fendi, and Ferragamo later, and even I felt shopped out.

"What's wrong, Flan?" my mom asked. "Do you think the Fendi blazer you bought is the wrong color?"

"No," I insisted. "I love it. I don't know, maybe the jet lag is still affecting me. I just got really tired."

"Take a load off." My dad gestured to the large courtyard full of café tables. "I'll order us a few lemon sodas and we'll people-watch your strength back."

It sounded like a great idea, and it did feel really great to sit down after all the running around we'd been doing. The people-watching was hilarious and fun too. Italians were certainly in love with their hot pinks and electric blues. But what stood out more was that they were also in love with each other. Literally. Everyone around us was a couple: young and old, short and tall, fabulously dressed and even more fabulously dressed. And every single one of them was making out. It was like I'd suddenly ended up in the capital of PDA-ville, and I was all alone. I closed my eyes and started rubbing my temples.

What was my problem today? I just couldn't get Alex out of my head. I remembered what SBB had mentioned the other day about Bianca, the Serbian breakup expert, and it started to make sense why people had to resort to such drastic measures. Was I going to be one of them?

I shuddered. No. This was only the beginning of my trip. I still had a whole week to make progress. All I needed was a good night's sleep, a can-do attitude, and a better day tomorrow.

Chapter 10

MOTHER KNOWS BEST

*W*hen the warm kiss of the Amalfi sunrise woke me up the next morning, my broken heart wasn't the first thing that popped into my head. Okay, it was the second, and the third, and the fourth—but at least I was making *some* progress!

On my bedside table, someone had left another gorgeous breakfast platter. Was it bad that I was getting used to this kind of special treatment? I was just about to pop a perfectly fuzzy apricot in my mouth when I heard the doorbell ring.

At first, I figured one of my parents would answer it, but after a minute, the doorbell was followed by a rough knock and the words, *"una casella da FedEx* for Signora Flan Flood."

The forgotten apricot plummeted from my fingers as I raced to pull on my robe. What if it was something from Alex? As I dashed to the front door of our villa,

I tried not to envision what he might have included in his "forgive me" care package. Black-and-white cookies from Pick a Bagel? That new Magnetic Fields CD we'd listened to at his apartment? A piece of jewelry from Bird, my favorite boutique in Brooklyn? No—it'd be better to be surprised.

But when I opened the door to the muscular Italian deliveryman, all he had in his hand was a tiny brown box. It seemed too tiny to make up for Alex's *huge* mistake. I gulped as I reached to sign the delivery slip. They *did* say good things came in small packages.

I glanced down at the handwriting on the box, and I hated to admit it, but my heart sank when I recognized it as Camille's. Instantly, a tidal wave of guilt hit me. I should be glad that I had friends who remembered to send me things even while they were having the time of their lives with their boyfriends in the most romantic city in the world.

With a sigh, I gave the FedEx man my best attempt at a smile and took my package out to the balcony. It was only eight o'clock, but our villa was already so quiet. My dad's golf clubs were gone from their spot in the corner and so was my mom's massive purple Longchamp shoulder bag. I guessed both my parents were already hard at "work."

Using the keys to our villa, I cut open the tape on the box to find a small gold-wrapped package and an envelope with my name on it. Inside the envelope was a group photo of the Paris crew, arm in arm at the top of the Eiffel Tower. All eight of them looked like they were having an amazing time—with big grins on their faces and big baguettes poking out of their tote bags. It would have been totally frameable if Camille hadn't drawn in a grinning stick figure next to where she stood in the photo. Her drawing had straight, shoulder-length hair, a crude depiction of the GPA binder in her hand, and the words *Flan in spirit* written above an arrow over her head. Despite myself, I was smiling when I read the card:

DEAR FLAN,

PARIS EST FANTASTIQUE, MAIS TU NOUS MANQUE! ARE YOU SURE YOU CAN'T JET UP FROM ITALY? WE MISS YOU DESPERATELY!

(It was right about then that I started to feel the tears well up again. Was my mom right? Was there no end to a woman's tear production? I read on.)

OKAY, OKAY, I KNOW YOU NEED THIS WEEK TO RECUPERATE, BUT WE'RE THINKING ABOUT YOU EVERY SECOND. IN FACT, I WAS THINKING ABOUT YOU THE WHOLE TIME I WAS READING THIS BOOK ON THE PLANE. READ IT—MAYBE IT'LL HELP. CALL ANYTIME.

EVERYONE SENDS *MILLES BISOUS*,

C.

I held the package in my hand. The silky wrapping paper was so pretty that I almost didn't want to rip it. Carefully, I pulled at the tape until the paper fell away and I could see the title of the book: *Feast, Fast, Fall*.

I opened the cover to read the jacket copy and started to understand why Camille had thought of me while she was reading—it was a memoir about a woman trying to get over a really bad breakup. It was sweet of Camille to think of me, but I wasn't sure it was going to do any good.

Occasionally, SBB would send me to the self-help section of one of the bookstores in my neighborhood when she was too paranoid of paparazzi to go herself. So I'd spent a lot of time flipping through the books on the shelf to find something suitable for her insanity du jour. But personally, I'd never been too into the self-help books for myself. Then again, I'd never really been through anything like this.

With no parents to entertain me, and no real way to get anywhere (after yesterday morning, I wasn't going to risk taking out the scooter on my own), I stepped back into my bedroom to grab the tray of breakfast food. I guessed I could just hunker down on the balcony, reading and eating the day away.

Only a few pages into the book, I was hooked. This woman really had the right idea. She wasn't trying to rush herself into getting over her breakup—in fact, she was totally indulging herself. A woman after my very own heart. She was in Italy; I was in Italy. She was stuffing her face with pizza; I was stuffing my face with *pane alla cioccolato*. Though pizza sounded really good—I wondered if any of the pizzerias in Sorrento delivered. Hmm . . .

"Yoo-hoo, darling!" I heard my mother's voice followed by the click of her stilettos on the marble floor.

I looked up from my book to see my mother, fully done up in snakeskin Derek Lam heels, a navy blue Calvin Klein bathing suit with matching cover-up, and the biggest straw hat I'd ever seen. She actually had to lift it up with both hands to make eye contact with me.

"Oh, hi Mom," I said sleepily.

"'Oh, hi Mom'?" she repeated. "What are you doing lazing around like this all alone? Come laze around with me—on the beach. I just had the most marvelous facial at Donatella's. I'll tell you all about it once we're spread out in the warm sun. And you can tell me all about what you've been up to!"

I yawned and settled back into my lounge chair. "You're looking at it," I said, reaching for another pastry. "There isn't really much more to tell."

"Then let's get out there and make some memories!" She grinned. "I know how you love the feel of the rushing waves at your back. I'll be your photographer—like the paparazzi. You can pretend you want your privacy, and I'll just snap away!"

"Eh, I'm pretty comfortable here." I shrugged. "Hey, do you know of any good pizza places that deliver? I was thinking of ordering in."

My mom cocked her head at me and reached over to read the title of my book. Her eyes narrowed into a squint.

"Oh, no, you don't," she said, shaking her finger at me.

"What?"

"I read that book. That woman gained thirty-five pounds when she was in Italy."

"But—I just—Alex—"

"I'm not saying don't enjoy the local cuisine to the fullest, but drowning yourself in delivery pizza because you're sad about a boy is no way to experience Italy. I won't let you wallow on a balcony all day. Put that book down and get your bathing suit on. Pronto!"

I wasn't used to my mom being such a drill sergeant. I kind of liked it. As much as I'd gotten used to the idea of daylong balcony wallowing, she did have a point. I put down the book and stood up.

"That's more like it," Mom said, giving me a quick shove toward my bedroom.

When we were comfortably seated on a giant terry cloth blanket under a huge green umbrella on the beach, my mom reached into her bag and pulled out a copy of just about every trashy magazine that existed, both in the States and in Italy.

"I know we can't really *read* the Italian tabloids," she said, shrugging, "But surely we can still enjoy the photos. Look at those pecs!"

I leaned in to check out the glossy centerfold of the Italian movie star, Giuseppe Gianni. I didn't recognize his face. I guessed he hadn't yet broken out onto the American silver screen—but if muscle mass meant anything in Hollywood, I imagined he was on his way.

Then, something just above the pages of the magazine caught my mom's eye.

"Look at that guy," she said, pointing at a real-live attractive bronzed muscleman walking along the beach in front of us. "I think he and Giuseppe must be on the same workout regimen."

I tried to laugh, but I didn't really feel like scoping out guys with my mom at the moment. Still, she was determined. She flipped up her sunglasses and rotated my chin back toward the Italian stallion, just as he dove into the water.

"What?" I said. "I see him." I was fully aware that I sounded sort of whiny, but I couldn't really help it.

"I'm trying to prove to you how many other gorgeous fish there are in the sea," my mom insisted.

"I guess I'm just not interested." I sighed and reached for my book again.

My mom sighed too and reached for her magazine.

For a moment we read in silence, but both of us could totally feel the tension. Finally, Mom threw down her magazine.

"This isn't working," she said, sounding upset. "I thought a little R and R with M and D would help, but clearly Italy just isn't the remedy."

"I'm sorry, Mom," I said, meeting her sad eyes. "I know you're trying."

"Don't apologize. But no mother likes to see her daughter fall into such a slump. Not when I could do something about it."

She scratched her head, then picked up her phone and typed a few thousand words in about a minute.

"What would you say to a flight to Thailand to visit Feb tonight?" she asked.

My eyes lit up. I'd never been to Asia.

"Maybe the pace is too slow for you here," she

continued. "Maybe what you need is to keep busy. And we know Feb. She'll put you right to work in one of those little rice shanties."

Her description was pretty funny, but actually, keeping busy with my bossy big sister did sound like it might take my mind off things.

"Anyway," Mom continued, "they're staying at the Four Seasons, so it's not like you'll have to rough it *that* much. What do you think? Sound good?"

I flung my arms around my mom and bobbed my head with more energy than I'd had in days.

"Sounds great!"

When I opened my eyes on Tuesday morning, I had no idea where I was. The room was dark and cold, and the bed was uncomfortably small. Everything around me was shaky, but I couldn't figure out why. Was this what an earthquake felt like? Did they even *have* earthquakes in Manhattan?

"The captain has turned on the 'fasten seat belt' sign, indicating our initial descent into Bangkok."

When the seat belt sign illuminated over my first-class seat on the small Alitalia plane, all the painful details came flooding back to me. I wasn't in Manhattan at all. I was on a plane to visit Feb in Thailand . . . because my mom was worried about my "slump" . . . because I was having a miserable time in Italy . . . because I'd just had my heart broken. Hmph, I would almost have preferred a minor earthquake.

How did the rest of my family keep up with where in

the world they were, when, and why? Jaunting around three continents in under a week had totally thrown me for a loop. But this was typical for the rest of the Floods, just like a walk in Central Park was for me.

On the bright side, at least my family was aware of my habits. They expected me to need a little extra hand-holding this week. After my mom had booked my plane ticket from Naples direct to Bangkok, I'd over-heard her on the phone with Feb. The phrase "she's in a fragile state" escaped her lips more than a few times.

The plan was for Feb to pick me up at the airport and take me back to our adjoining rooms at the Four Seasons. I pushed through the throngs of people at baggage claim, thinking how glad I was going to be to see a familiar, sisterly face in the crowd. This place was crazy! I could barely breathe, let alone see over the heads of all the men in business suits, shouting into their phones, to find my luggage.

I turned on my phone to see if Feb had left me a voice mail about where to find her, but instead, I found her text message.

SOOO SORRY—DEBACLE AT THE RICE MARSH, COULDN'T GET OUT IN TIME TO MEET YOUR FLIGHT. A LONG-HAIRED MAN NAMED BENJY IS ON THE LOOKOUT FOR YOU. HE'LL TAKE YOU TO THE COMPOUND. I PROMISE TO MAKE THIS UP TO YOU SOON!

I looked around the terminal nervously. No Feb to meet me, and now I was supposed to find some stranger in the midst of all these other strangers? This was certainly not very good for my fragile state!

I crossed my arms and bit my lip and was just about to fire back a cranky text to Feb, when I felt a tap on my shoulder. I turned around to find a lanky Thai man with shoulder-length black hair and a ripped T-shirt that said *Peace Corps*, but that looked surprisingly cool and vintagey.

"You must be February's sister," he said, showing two deep dimples when he smiled.

"How'd you know?" I said. People were almost always surprised when they found out Feb and I were sisters. We couldn't look—or act—more unalike.

He glanced down at a scrap of paper, then held it out for me to see my sister's handwriting:

HOT BLONDE, PROBABLY DRESSED IN ALL BLACK, WILL BE BITING HER LIP AND CROSSING HER ARMS BY THE TIME YOU FIND HER.

"Oh," I said, looking down at my Twenty8Twelve black turtleneck and black Marc Jacobs jeans. I quickly uncrossed my arms and made a mental note to stop biting my lip in the future.

"She also wrote out a description of your luggage," Benjy said. "I hope you don't mind—I saw it come around the conveyor, so I grabbed it." He pointed at the ground, and there was my burgundy Brix duffel. Relief washed over me. I decided to forgive Feb just a little bit for sending such a helpful guide in her place.

A train, rickshaw, and canoe ride later, I was even gladder to have Benjy around. From the window of the train, he pointed out the clustered buildings making up downtown, and even gave a few good recommendations for dance clubs along the way. Sitting next to me on the rickshaw, as we got farther away from the hectic inner city, he gave me the history of the rice marshes where he and Feb and Kelly were all working. As we climbed into the canoe and he rowed us through the misty water of the Chao Phraya River, he explained how the terrain had changed during the monsoon seasons the past few years. As we floated past the bamboo reeds, the scenery was phenomenal and unlike anything I'd ever seen before, but I was starting to wonder if I'd ever reach my sister.

"There you are—finally!" a familiar voice called from the bank of the river. Feb was standing on a short wooden dock, waving both her arms over her head. She was wearing a simple black smock and baggy jeans, and her hair was cropped super short. Last month's red dye was already growing out, so half her hair was her natural dark brown, but the tips were a muted red color. My sister looked nothing like the Feb I'd had lunch with last week, but it was still so good to see her.

"So," I said, after we'd hugged and I had a chance to finally take in the thatched roof hut behind her. "This is the most unusual Four Seasons I've ever seen."

Feb looked confused, then flung her hand dismissively in the air. "That's a little white lie so Mom doesn't totally freak about the Peace Corps thing. You know, Flan, you can't *always* tell her the truth."

But when she saw the surprised look on my face, she quickly added, "Forget I said that, bad advice. Anyway, you're here now and that's what matters." She put her arm around my shoulder and led me to the bungalow.

"It's a little rustic, but it's off the grid, and it's really close to our work quarters, so . . ." She trailed off, pulling back a beaded curtain to expose a small bedroom. Inside was a large window facing the river, and no furniture other than simple pallet on the floor and a mosquito net hanging from the ceiling.

"Oh God, you're stunned silent," Feb said, sounding nervous. "This must be quite a shock after the villa treatment you probably got in Sorrento. Do you hate it?"

"Are you kidding?" I said. "This might be coolest place I've ever stayed."

"See, I told you Flan could handle it," Kelly said, coming up behind Feb to give me a hug. He was also dressed in a simple smock and casual jeans. He'd carried in my duffel bag and set it down on the floor.

"You are aware that your mom told us to put you right to work, aren't you?" he said, with a sly smirk on his face.

"Kelly's kidding, Flan." Feb sighed, exasperated. "We're not going to put you to work—are you crazy? We want you to enjoy yourself here."

"But Mom said I need to keep busy, to keep my mind off of—"

"Trust me, there's plenty to keep you busy here—and keep your mind off of he who shall remain nameless—*without* sticking you in a rice field. Look," she said, reaching into the pocket of her smock. "I made you a whole list of things to do."

She handed me a sheet of paper with her signature messy scrawl. The list was broken down by category: restaurants, shopping, and sacred places. I wanted to see everything—I didn't even know where to start. Luckily, at that moment, my stomach growled, pulling my eyes to the restaurant section first.

"Tom Yam Kung sounds great," I said, thinking

that if a restaurant was named after my favorite spicy lemongrass soup, it had to be delicious.

"It's the best in the city." Feb nodded. "You have to go there—in fact, you should go tonight."

"*I* should go?" I repeated. "Won't *we* go there together?"

Feb shot Kelly a look and scratched her head. "Thing is, Flan, we're doing this fast. Just for another thirty-six hours—don't look so shocked, it's really restorative."

"Let me get this straight," I said. "You're not going to eat . . . at all?"

Kelly piped up: "But don't let that stop you from enjoying yourself."

Didn't Mom send me to here to shake me *out* of the *Feast, Fast, Fall* mind-set?

"Here's what you do," Feb said. "Take our canoe across the river, hail yourself a rickshaw into town, and have it drop you off at Khao San Road."

"By myself?" I asked.

"It's a total party zone," Feb said. "You'll have a blast."

Before I knew it, both of them were guiding me back down the dock, where a row of old canoes was moored. Feb handed me an oar and said, "You sure you're going to be okay?"

I forced myself to nod, even though I was anything but sure. I didn't want to get in the way of their fast, or make them wish they hadn't agreed to put me up.

"Don't stay out too late," Feb warned, as if I'd be rocking the clubs till dawn.

"That's right," Kelly agreed. "We have big plans for you tomorrow." And with that, Feb gave the canoe a gentle shove with her foot and sent me down the misty river by myself.

This was crazy, and terrifying, and . . . really freaking cool. As I paddled down the river (something I hadn't done since Camp Starlight) I tried to mentally recap how I, Flan Flood, had ended up here. It didn't seem possible—or real.

When I heard the special "Paper Planes" ringtone that I'd set for Camille—hallelujah!—I seized the phone from my pocket. Hopefully there were no laws about canoeing and talking on your phone at the same time.

"Camille?" I said.

"Flan?" she said.

"Please tell me I'm not dreaming," we both said at the same time.

"You first," I said.

"I'm in Jade Moodswing's atelier! Help! I'm addicted to couture. What about you?"

I struggled between wanting to ask Camille a million questions about Jade's new line and wanting to spill everything about my trip to Thailand.

"I'm rowing myself down the Chao Phraya River in Bangkok," I said finally.

"Ha-ha. So, tell me—how are the Italian men?" she asked.

"No, seriously, I'm in Bangkok. Italy . . . wasn't working," I said, using my mom's expression. "So I flew out last night—"

"Flan, you're breaking up!" I looked down at my phone and saw that I was just about out of range. Before the phone completely cut out, I heard bits of Camille shouting. "You better write me a long e-mail pronto, and you'd better send pics of you having fun!"

I sighed and hung up the phone, just as tip of the canoe nudged the bank of the river. A cluster of rickshaw drivers were leaning up against a bungalow, waiting to take people into the city.

"You need a ride, miss?" three of them jumped to ask.

I thought about Camille yelling at me to have fun, about SBB's looming deadline for getting over Jony, and about my mom insisting that keeping busy would help. I took a deep breath, stepped out of the canoe, and said, "Take me to Khao San Road."

Mooooo. Mooooooo!"

Wednesday morning, I awoke on my mosquito-netted pallet to the sounds of a cattle stampede.

"Feb?" I called, struggling to pull myself out of bed after what felt like a very short night of sleep. I guessed I was still out of whack from the time zone changes. "I thought you were working on a rice farm," I said. "Not a dairy farm."

When I pushed back the beaded curtain separating my bedroom from the main living space of the bungalow, I saw that Feb and Kelly were seated on the floor. Their eyes were closed and their legs were folded in this crazy yogic position. Just as I opened my mouth to ask where the cow pen was, both Feb and Kelly opened their mouths and let out a sonorous *moooooo*.

Oh. That's where the cow pen was.

"Very nice. Keep breathing, the answer is within you," a very soft male voice chanted.

I hadn't even noticed anyone else in the room, but once my eyes fell on the small, round man in the corner, it seemed like an easy mistake. He was wearing a knee-length linen shirt and loose slacks, both the same color as the walls. His wrinkled skin bunched up to hide his features. He could easily have been a hundred years old. Who was this dude?

I tried to tiptoe toward the bathroom to brush my teeth, but the sound of my steps on the dirt floor caused one of Feb's eyes to pop open. When she looked at me, she lost her balance and fell out of her meditation position.

"February, you have broken your nirvana," the man said.

"I'm sorry, Guru," Feb said, sounding more reverent than I'd ever heard her sound when she spoke to my parents. "I sensed another presence and broke my concentration." She pointed at me. "This is my younger sister, Flan."

I was starting to feel like all I'd done since I got to Thailand was interrupt my sister and her new Zen way of life. I was about to duck into the bathroom in shame, when Kelly waved me over to the floor.

"Come join us for the breakfast mediation," he said. "You're just in time for one last mantra."

These two were substituting meditation for breakfast! But I guessed I wouldn't be opposed to combining the two. The few times I'd gone to yoga with SBB had been really chill and relaxing, and you know what they say: when in Thailand . . .

I plopped down on the floor between them, trying to fold my legs up accordingly. Okay, I was just going to have to settle for preschool pretzel style.

The guru started walking in circles around our cluster on the floor. He was repeating the same Sanskrit phrases, so softly that it almost sounded like he was speaking to himself. Feb whispered occasional translations to me, and I tried to sink into the zone. But I was getting hungrier by the mantra—and eager to find an Internet café or someplace I could send Camille a real update. There was so much I needed to spill. I kept opening my eyes to see if anyone else was finished chanting. Every once in a while, the guru would catch my eye and give me a soft, smiling shake of the head.

By the end of the session, twenty pad-thai-on-the-brain minutes later, Feb and Kelly's faces were beading with sweat. Both of them belted out the same final mantra at the same haunting pitch. When they opened their eyes, they looked at each other and shared a smile.

When Feb finally stood up to get a glass of water, I followed her to the kitchen.

"So what was all this moo stuff about?" I asked, grabbing a bottle of water from the tiny fridge for myself.

"*Mu*," she corrected. "We were exercising our inner questioner. You use *mu* to respond to something irrelevant. Roughly, it means 'un-ask the question.' But, you know, in a groovy, peaceful sort of way."

I nodded. "So, if I were to ask you if there was a good place for coffee and a New York bagel around here—"

"*Mu*," Feb interrupted, cracking a smile. "I have to change the subject before I start thinking too hard about an everything with jalapeño cream cheese from H&H." She sighed. "So how was last night?"

"Fun," I lied, thinking about how lonely I'd felt sitting at the restaurant all by myself, and how even though there were all these cool street vendors to explore, I'd basically come straight home after having a bowl of soup.

"You're bored," Feb said, reading my tone. "Listen, I promised you a good time, and I'm going to show you one."

I grinned. When Feb said that, it usually meant shopping by day to prepare for a killer party by night.

"Cool," I said. "So where should we brunch? I know there's no Orsay, but—"

Feb held up a hand. "Sorry, Flan. Our fast ends at sundown. And I have to work in the fields until then. Hey, quit frowning. We'll throw down tonight."

"But—" I started to say, imagining another day of wandering listlessly around town.

"Before you get all melancholy on me," Feb said, "Kelly thought you might want to spend some time with our guru."

"Huh?" What on earth would I do with a guru?

"He's a really good listener," Feb insisted. "Maybe you could talk things out."

I looked over at the guru, who had Kelly lying on the floor with both of his legs in a pretzel position behind his head. It didn't look like there was a whole lot of listening going on, just a whole lot of physical strain. But if Feb was going to be at the rice paddies all day, what else did I have to do?

"I'm not going to have to do any Cirque du Soleil–style positions, am I?" I said.

"*Mu.*" Feb laughed, and brought me over to the guru.

An hour later, I was sitting at the top of a cliff, looking down at all of Bangkok, which seemed so far away.

After Feb and Kelly hosed me down with some crazy Thai mosquito repellent and outfitted me in a pair of Feb's army green waterproof boots, the guru led me up a steep trail, through what felt like an enchanted forest, across two rushing streams, and finally to a clearing at the top of a cliff.

"This is a space of total serenity," he said in the same even tone of voice. "I hope you will find it comfortable." He motioned for me to take a seat on a rock facing the cliff's edge, and together we looked out at the view. I was watching the slow movement of canoes and cargo boats down the river, when the guru took my hand and slid something inside it.

I looked down to find a red stone on a red rope. I'd seen a lot of these amulets for sale on the streets last night, but I hadn't stopped to look closely at any of them yet. This one featured a carving of a small, smiling Buddha figure, who didn't look unlike the guru. When I looked up at him, he took my hand and flipped the amulet over to the other side. I held it up to the light to read a tiny inscription on the stone:

Protection from your feelings of betrayal.

"You came here looking for answers," the guru said.

"Actually," I said, twisting my fingers around the necklace, "I came here because my mom thought—"

He put his hand up as if to apologize for interrupting. "But you *are* here, and you *are* seeking answers. Your sister says you have had a betrayal," he said evenly, as if it were totally normal for my sister to fill in this stranger on the intimate details of my heart.

I looked out at the sun, which was starting to peek over the trees lining the river, and I couldn't help wondering what kind of rare birds were perched in their branches. Alex would know. He'd have a book, and his binoculars, and . . . The guru was still staring at me.

"If you are looking for the fleeting hornbill, you'll find him there," he said, pointing a finger at the low bough of a tree where a wild black and yellow bird took flight. "But just like everything else in life, his perch is fleeting."

"I really liked him, Guru," I said softly. "Not the hornbill—my boyfriend. Ex-boyfriend."

"Just as the sun and the stars are in motion, so is your pain. Relief will come."

Clearly this guy had never met SBB. He might have been very wise in some circles, but he had no idea that in my near future, there was either a party—or an appointment with Berserk Bianca. I didn't want to disagree with the guru, who had a really sweet disposition and an impressive grasp on local wildlife, but for my own sake, I had to disagree. Recalling the jpeg that SBB had sent me of Bianca—drawn cheeks, severe hairline, terrifying eyes—I knew I didn't have *time* to give it time!

"With all due respect, Guru," I said, surprising myself with my boldness, "I disagree. I can't just let this heartbreak run its course. I'm sorry, but it wouldn't be me."

"'*Me*'?" the guru repeated, seeming to mentally chew on the word. "That is not a Buddhist outlook." He patted my shoulder. "But you have a strong will. I like that."

"So you don't disapprove of my trying to move on?" I asked.

"*Mu*," he said, so solemnly it took me a second to realize that he was making a joke.

"Wear the amulet," he said, standing up from his rock on the mountain. "You may choose not to take the Buddhist approach, but the Buddha will still watch over you."

I slipped the amulet over my head and shook the guru's hand. "Luckily," I joked, "red is totally my color."

After we parted ways, I decided to stay in the place of serenity for a little longer. I pulled out my phone and texted SBB:

WHIRLWIND WEEK. DIVERTED TO THAILAND TO HANG WITH FEB. BUT DON'T WORRY—OPERATION GET OVER JONY STILL IN FULL SWING. BETTER DUST OFF YOUR PARTY MANOLOS FOR MY RETURN. HOW'S THE WEIGHT GAIN GOING?

The speed of SBB's response made me feel like the amulet was working already:

GREETINGS FROM IN-N-OUT BURGER IN L.A. JR SAYS I'M IN THE SEVENTIETH PERCENTILE FOR MY WEIGHT CLASS. I WILL NOT LET IT GET ME DOWN! GLAD THAILAND SEEMS TO BE BEEFING UP YOUR HEART. SHOULD I KEEP BIANCA'S NUMBER ON SPEED DIAL . . . JUST IN CASE?

Gulp.

Chapter 13
A NOT-SO-THAI-RIFFIC TURN OF EVENTS

$\mathcal{I}$ need seventy-two jumbo paper lanterns, with the energy-saving lightbulbs, and I need them delivered *now*."

There was the sister I knew and loved! When I stepped into the long open bar on the top floor of the Oriental Hotel, I was greeted by Feb, pacing the hardwood floor on her phone. She was still the same girl—she'd just been hiding under that organically woven paper bag of a dress for the past few days.

She'd sent me an urgent text to meet her at the hotel at four-thirty on Wednesday afternoon. The fast was just about over, and we were all gearing up for the big party she was throwing to honor a good monsoon week on the rice marsh. Quite a change from the parties she used to host in honor of a friend's movie premiere or club opening, but a party nonetheless. I was excited just to be out on the town and spending some

113

nonyoga time with my sister. But I was also very excited that the party was being held at the city's swank Oriental Hotel. It had been around forever, and over the years had seen all of Thailand's glitterati spin through its golden doors.

Speaking of spinning, Feb was starting to make me dizzy with all her pacing back and forth.

"Feb, can I—"

"Flan, I haven't eaten in seventy-two hours and fourteen minutes and Idon'tevenknowhowmanyseconds. I really can't deal with—"

"I was just going to ask if I could help with anything for the party," I jumped in before she said something she regretted.

Feb paused, snapped her phone shut, and said, "Actually, there is something you can do."

Before I knew it, she had led me into the walk-in fridge in the large gleaming hotel kitchen. She stopped in front of six boxes full of coconuts and six boxes of the biggest, ripest mangos I'd ever seen in my life.

"Ouch," I said, when Feb slapped my hand after I reached into the box to examine one of the fantastically pink pieces of fruit.

"Look, don't touch," Feb said brusquely. "They're for tonight. Ugh, I've got a million things to do," she said, looking down at her PDA, which looked so out of place in her henna-tattooed hand. "Let's see. We *have* to have a signature cocktail. You can come up with something on the fly, right?"

It was a good thing I wasn't holding a mango, because I would have dropped it. "Me? Bartending?"

"Not bar*tending*," she said, sounding only slightly impatient. "Bar *inspiring*. Isn't that what you do? Patch mentioned something you whipped up for some Thoney party. . . ."

Camille and I had concocted a really delicious Virgiltini for January's Virgil event. And my friends always said that I made the best acai spritzers (the secret was to line the rim of the glass with real dried acai berries crushed with sugar). But I'd never stopped to think about the fact that I actually had a gift for concocting delicious and refreshing drinks. I loved that Feb made it sound like cocktail commander was my obvious terrain.

"We just need a pretty face behind the drink. It'll market better," she said.

"You can take a girl out of a Manhattan PR firm . . ." I joked.

"Ha-ha," Feb said, motioning for me to help her carry a box of coconuts. "So what do you think?"

"Well," I said, looking down at the boxes of fruit.

115

"In this kind of sticky heat, people want something light."

"So no coconut milk?" Feb asked. Her face seemed to fall. We *were* looking at six huge crates of coconuts.

"I've got it," I said finally, thinking of what my friend Ramsey, the captain of my field hockey team, was always telling us to drink before practice. "We'll go with nature's biggest thirst quencher: coconut *water*! Blended with ice and mint and a dollop of mango puree. We can call it . . . Thai-riffic."

"She's a genius," Feb said to the team of Thai chefs putting on their aprons. "Okay, now we divide and conquer," she said, turning back to me. "I'll make sure the music's cued and the candles are lit. You find the bartenders and spread your refreshing gospel, okay?"

"Just one question," I said, looking down at myself and realizing one very big hitch in the plan. When I'd showed up in my jeans and casual Theory tee, I'd envisioned having time to make it home and change. "Am I going to wear this to the party?"

Feb threw her head back and started laughing hysterically, telling me all I needed to know.

A half hour later, I had just made a sample virgin Thai-riffic cocktail for the bartender to taste, when Feb shoved a hanger under my nose. I held it out in front of me to examine the short silk sheath dress. The cut was simple; the print was anything but. It was white with dashes of black, hot pink, bright green, and dark red. If I squinted, I could almost make out a graphic print of Marilyn Monroe. It was cool (sorta) and edgy (very), but the dress was not at all me.

"I picked it out for you in the shop downstairs. It matches your amulet," Feb said, sounding proud of herself. "And it complements my dress!" she said, holding up a similarly loud blue and white splatter-painted T-shirt dress. Yikes.

Usually Feb had impeccable taste when it came to clothes. Maybe she was just out of shopping practice? But she looked so busy, standing there crossing off things on her electronic to-do list. I knew she'd flip if I asked for a new dress.

I looked past my sister at a group of three Thai girls about my age. They were giggling in front of the elevator. For a second, they reminded me of me and my friends, and I got a not-in-Paris pang. Then I realized that all these girls were wearing something very similar to what Feb had just picked out. Hmm.

I wasn't the type to follow trends that I didn't genuinely adore, but then again, it was only one night, and if other people were wearing the style, at least my crazy Marilyn dress wouldn't make me the laughingstock of Bangkok.

"It's great," I said to Feb, slipping into the bath-room to pull on the dress.

By the time I gave myself a quick touch-up (loos-ened side ponytail, shimmery Urban Decay highlighter rimmed around my eyes, and DuWop matte pink lip-stick), the ballroom of the hotel was already filling up with guests. It seemed really early, but then I remem-bered that Feb and Kelly got up at the crack of dawn to hit the rice paddies, so most of their guests were prob-ably on the same schedule. The sun hadn't even set, and people were already lined up to order my Thai-riffics. If taste in cocktails was any indication, I guessed the party was off to a pretty good start.

Feb was still in intense-planning mode, and she had Kelly handling the spillover chores, so both of them were rushing around making sure the lanterns were hung, the Thai dancers on time, the stereo system set up. They looked so frazzled, and I loved attending to these last-minute details. Over and over, I asked them if I could help, and over and over, Feb insisted that I get "out there" and enjoy myself.

So I tried. I milled around the room, sampling bar-becue fish skewers and spicy vegetarian dumplings. I stifled a yawn. I leaned up against the bar to enjoy the view of the city from the twenty-seventh floor of the hotel. I looked at my reflection in the window, yawning.

From this perspective, unlike me, Bangkok never seemed to rest. But there had to be people out there doing normal things, just sitting down to dinner with their family, or going to see a movie . . . or nursing a broken heart. From the outside, you'd never be able to tell. It made me wonder whether anyone at this party could tell what I was going through.

"Flan? Is that you?" a familiar voice said behind me. I turned around to see Arno Wildenburger standing with his arms extended. Arno was an old friend of Patch's, but I'd hung out with him enough times that I felt like we were friends in our own right, too. The last time I'd seen him, he had hooked me up with tickets to see the Magnetic Fields' secret show under the Brooklyn Bridge. It was strange to see a familiar smile in this sea of new faces, but Arno was impossible to miss, especially in this crowd. His dark hair practically gleamed with the Frédéric Fekkai glossing gel he bought by the case, and his watches (one for every day of the week) were always the size of a hockey puck. He'd always just seemed like a normal kid to me, but tonight he looked so New York.

"You look sooo Bangkok in that dress," he said, giving me an approving nod. "Way to go."

"Thanks, Arno." I stepped in to give him a quick kiss on the cheek, not expecting him to pull me in for such a tight squeeze. "What are you doing here?" I asked his shoulder, since that was what my face was mashed into.

"Looking for you," he said, giving me a super-cheesy wink. "No, really, I'm just stopping though on my back from Sydney, hanging with Patch, but I didn't know I was going to going to have the pleasure of buying the most beautiful of all the Floods a drink."

I laughed, rolling my eyes. "I was just in Italy, and the men there can get away with saying stuff like that, but aren't you supposed to be an icy cool Manhattanite?"

It was good to see Arno. It was just his personality to be forward, so I could give him a hard time without worrying that it meant anything.

"You're right, that was embarrassing," he said, putting his arm around me. "Why don't I buy you a drink and you can tell me all about Italy . . . and whether you're finally single so I can ask you out."

My face fell. It was completely involuntary and instantaneous, but Arno picked up on it in a second.

"Uh-oh. That's a boy-trouble face if I've ever seen one. What's his name?"

"Actually," I said, pushing him away, "I don't really want to talk about it."

"What's his name?"

"Alex." I sighed at last. "Alex Altfest."

Arno crossed his arms over his chest and cocked his head at me. "Please tell me you're not all broken up over *Alex Altfest*."

"Why not?" I blurted out. "You know him?"

"I know the kid. And let me tell you, Flan, he ain't worth one pretty little tear of yours."

The mention of my tears must have had some sort of physical response, because I could feel them welling up. Who did Arno think he was, saying Alex wasn't worth it?

"If he's not worth it, then why am I—" I cut myself off.

"Flan, come on." He reached for my shoulder, but I pulled away. His fingers snagged on the chain of my amulet and I felt the sharp tug of it catching around my neck. A second later, it snapped off. The glossy stone Buddha cracked in two clean pieces on the floor.

"Crap," Arno muttered. "Where'd you get that? I'll buy you another one."

"You can't *buy* me another one Arno. That's the point of the amulet—it's not replaceable. It's valuable because of who gives it to you and why. And I don't want one from you." I knew it was unfair to go off on him, but at this point, I couldn't stop. "I don't need the necklace anyway, just as much as I don't need you telling me who or what to cry over. What I need . . ." What did I need? "What I need is to get out of here," I said, nearly tripping over the line of Thai-riffic orderers and rushing out of the bar.

This party was a disaster, and if I didn't find a bathroom quickly, I was going to cry in front of the still-giggling elevator girls.

I ducked behind a Buddha statue and collapsed on a bench out of view from the partygoers. I wanted to call my friends, but I didn't know if I could bear to be reminded that they were all having a blast with their boys. I already felt so far away from them. I pulled out my phone to find two text messages, one from Camille and one from SBB.

Camille's said:

THINKING OF YOU FROM THE TOP OF THE CENTRE POMPIDOU. XANDER SAYS ALEX IS AT THE KNICKS GAME TONIGHT—NOT THAT YOU SHOULD WASTE YOUR TIME THINKING ABOUT HIM. JUST THOUGHT YOU SHOULD KNOW THAT HE'S STILL IN THE CITY, AND YOU'RE OFF SEEING THE WORLD!

I guess it was sweet of Camille to put it like that, but all her text did was fill me with questions. We used to go to Knicks games together. We'd sit in his family's box seats and order oysters from the Grand Central Oyster Bar and try to shoot oysters every time LeBron James shot a three-pointer. Who was he taking to the games now? Before the word *Cookie* could fully form in my head, I opened SBB's text:

AFTER A WEEK OF HOLLYWOOD MEETINGS, JR REWARDS ME WITH AN ORDER TO WEIGHT-TRAIN IN SYDNEY. HMPH! I KNOW YOU'RE BANGKOK-ROCKING, BUT OZ ISN'T SOOO FAR FROM YOUR HOOD, IS IT? WANNA POP DOWN AND HELP LITTLE OLD ME BECOME NOT-SO-LITTLE OLD ME??? PLEASE???? BIANCA WILL BE HAPPY TO JOIN US IF NEEDED. . . .

Hmm, SBB might be joking, since just popping down to Australia was a pretty ridiculous idea. But then I remembered Patch and Agnes's presentation. Would they still be in Sydney? Only the world's most strings-pulling travel agent could work this kind of flight-reservation miracle. I crossed my fingers as I dialed my mom. . . .

Chapter 14

After one last night sleeping under the mosquito nets, and one final canoe ride down the Chao Phraya, I was back at the airport, holding a last-minute plane ticket to Sydney.

I'd spent the whole morning apologizing profusely to Feb for my behavior (namely for blowing into their no-stress zone only to turn around and dash off, leaving a trail of tears). Not surprisingly, Feb would have none of it.

"Will you shut up already?" she said, kissing me good-bye at the airport. "You'll have much more fun down under with Patch. It's impossible to sulk in Sydney. Frowning is practically illegal. Now get on the plane. Call me when you're over he who shall not be named." She practically shoved me through the gate.

Following her last orders, I trooped down the runway toward the small first-class-only jet. When I found my window seat (thanks, Mom!), I sank into the smooth leather recliner, happy to see that there was a computer screen on the seat back in front of me. My iPhone reception had been so spotty in Thailand, it felt like years since I'd been able to check my e-mail, and I was dying for the extended version of the news from Paris. But the first thing I did when I logged on was a quick scan to see whether the Jerk of New York had decided to apologize (negative . . . hmph!). My spirits lifted when I saw the subject line of Camille's e-mail: THIS IS A LONG ONE; SIT DOWN. I snuggled into my down airline blanket, glad that Feb had insisted on taking me to the airport extra early so she could get back in time for her session with the guru. Now I had plenty of time to read before takeoff:

CHÈRE FLAN,

HAVE FINALLY RECOVERED FROM YOUR CRAZY JET-SETTING NEWS ABOUT THAILAND. MUST KNOW EVERYTHING! ARE YOU SWIMMING IN TOM YAM KUNG SOUP? ARE YOU BUDDHIST YET? WHAT ARE THEY WEARING IN BANGKOK?

It was funny, I'd been sort of bummed thinking about how I hadn't given Thailand much of a shot before I jumped on the first plane out of town, but reading Camille's e-mail, I was pleasantly surprised to have answers to all of her questions. I *had* tasted real tom yam kung, and I *did* have a memorable Buddhist moment. I even had the freaky Marilyn Monroe dress to prove how wild the fashion was. My short visit had exposed me to some really amazing new things.

I was feeling pretty good about myself until I got to Camille's next paragraph, where she launched into a series of questions about how I was doing re Jony. Of course, she had to ask—she was my best friend—but I didn't want to sink into that particular depression at the moment. So I just glossed over it and started reading again when she switched subjects.

Finally, this was the good stuff—a long description of what everyone had been eating (lots and lots of almond croissants), how many boutiques she'd spotted Jade Moodswing couture in (six), and how many times Morgan had gotten pissy because the daily half-hour rain shower was making her hair frizz (eleven). She also detailed this great lost-in-translation anecdote about Xander being chased down the street by a crazy French woman wielding a cast-iron pot, all because he'd accidentally called her a cow while trying to ask if she knew where he could find a good hamburger in her neighborhood.

I was laughing so hard that tears were rolling

down my face (oh yeah, I remembered these—the *good* kind of tears!), when a soothing voice overhead said:

"Well, at least I know she's got a sense of humor. That's always a good sign."

I looked up to lock eyes with a tall guy a few years older than me. He was a dangerous combination of Zac Efron and Christian Bale, with an Aussie accent to boot. He lifted a bag into the overhead compartment and slid into the seat next to me.

"I'm Dave," he said, giving me a very manly handshake. "We'll be each other's entertainment for the next nine hours."

Dave had shiny light brown hair that he had to keep shaking out of his dark hazel eyes. He was really tan, with a splash of freckles across his nose and a smile that seemed to spread through every one of his gorgeous features. If this guy was from Sydney, I understood what Feb meant when she said that frowning was culturally illegal.

"I'm Flan," I said, smiling too.

"And you're flying from Thailand to Sydney," he said, scratching his chin, "to meet up with your boyfriend? Oh, I can see that was the wrong question. On some sort of modeling junket, right?"

As the flight attendants closed the cabin doors and

the plane pushed back from the runway, Dave seemed to be sizing me up.

"Not exactly." I laughed, feeling myself turn red. "My brother's in Sydney and my friend's meeting me there." Usually, I would have left it there, but even though Dave was a stranger, there was something really trustworthy about his face. I was surprised to find myself saying, "As for the boyfriend part, I guess you could say I'm flying *away* from him. We just broke up."

Two Shirley Temples and an assorted-nut-and-cheese platter later, I'd given Dave the entire rundown. Not just the breakup story with Alex, but also the story of my whirlwind spring break. I even offered up the details of the looming threat of Bianca, which, when I showed him the photo SBB had sent, made both of us wince.

"Let me get this straight—you're traveling to three continents in nine days to get over one guy?"

I nodded, laughing to hear it phrased so succinctly.

"That reminds me of a card trick I know," Dave said, reaching into his pocket for a deck of cards. "You didn't take me for an excellent magician, did you?"

I shook my head and Dave proceeded to show me the most elaborate card trick I'd ever seen, involving three queens, the nine of hearts, and a joker. After he bowled me over with a few more tricks, I decided to show off my skills and beat him at a few games of gin rummy. When the captain announced that we were flying over New Zealand, it reminded Dave of this song on the new Bob Dylan album, so we biPodded for a little while. After that, we flipped through the movie channels and realized both SBB and Danny Tumble, an Aussie actor friend of Dave's, had cameos in *Arctic Lightning*. It was only when the captain turned on the seat belt sign to indicate we were landing that I realized I was having more fun on this airplane than I'd had all week on the ground in Italy and in Thailand.

"This is why I love long flights," Dave said, giving me that contagious smile. "By the time we land, we'll have already been on three dates."

"Oh, I get it," I said coyly. "Picking up girls on planes is your thing."

I phrased it as a joke, but I was also really hoping that Dave would insist it wasn't true. Luckily, he laughed.

"Yep, last flight, I met a lovely screeching infant. She really opened up to me, but then"—he mimicked a sniffle—"she never called."

"You just never know with babies, do you?" I joked.

It had been so long since I'd looked at another guy.

I couldn't believe how easy it was to fall right back into flirting. Dave and I smiled at each other and didn't say anything for a moment. Then he reached into his bag and took out his phone.

"Speaking of calling people," he said, "I'd say it's time for the obligatory number swap. Don't look so surprised—you're going to be in Sydney for a few days; I live in Sydney. It's only natural."

My heart picked up. Was I really going to give out my number to a guy I just met on the plane? What would my friends say? This wasn't the first time this week that I realized how much I needed them.

"In case you need more convincing, I happen to have a pretty sweet beach house in Coogee," Dave continued. "Don't you want to end your whirlwind tour on a high note?"

A brief vision of the Thoney girls flashed into my head. They'd be screaming their heads off for me to thrust my number at this gorgeous Aussie guy.

So I did.

Chapter 15

*F*irst I saw the FLANNIE-BANANIE sign quaking frantically in the air at the Sydney airport terminal. Then I saw the body holding it absolutely lose control when I came into view. SBB threw her arms up, accidentally tossing her handmade sign into the face of an elderly Japanese tourist. She started running toward me.

"Ohmygodiamsooooooooogladtoseeyou!" we both screamed at the exact same time, throwing our arms around each other. We jumped up and down in the embrace a few times before I realized that something was very different about my tiny starlet best friend.

She wasn't so tiny anymore.

On anyone else, a few extra pounds might not have made much of a difference, but because SBB's base weight had been next to nothing, even one week's worth of bulk was a very big deal.

131

"Whoa, SBB, have you been taking 'roids?" I asked, only sort of joking when I pulled back to examine her suddenly ripped biceps.

"No way," she scoffed. "Protein shakes and dumb-bells." When she shrugged dismissively, I could actually make out clearly defined delts (delts?!) through her layered Velvet tank tops.

"Well, it's working," I said, watching in awe as the former lightweight scooped up my massive Balenciaga carry-on as if it were stuffed with feathers instead of heavy books and magazines. "Which way to the gun show?" I joked.

"Flan," she said, putting on her serious face, "Australia is actually a very civilized place. It's not all hunting and bushmen."

"No," I said, shaking my head. "I was making a joke. You know, muscles, guns? Yours are enormous, by the way."

"Not enormous enough!" she said, suddenly putting on the fierce. "They always say the early mass is the easiest to put on. What if I peaked prematurely? What if I never get to gladiatrix stature? What if—"

She was interrupted by a loud beeping sound coming from her massive Prada pocket watch.

"Two-fifteen," she muttered to herself, turning

off the alarm. "It's time for my energy-bar-and-gel combo."

As the rush of other passengers scooted around us, I watched with horror as SBB pulled out a Kate Spade cosmetics case stuffed with the kinds of inedible snacks they always sell at GNCs. She ripped into a hefty white-wrapped bar that seemed to be about the same consistency as the compost heap Feb started making us keep in the backyard of our brownstone. SBB devoured the whole bar in four large gulps, then washed it down (if that term can be applied) with a small capsule of gel, whose packaging read *Energy Glide*.

Throughout the whole gruesome scene, the look on her face was one of absolute torture. She grimaced as she swallowed down the last of the Energy Glide, wiped her mouth daintily with a tissue, then turned to smile at me.

"Well, that's over," she said, looking back down at her watch. "At least for another forty-five minutes. Shall we go see about your bags?"

I nodded, still a little dazed by what I'd just witnessed. As we took the escalator down to baggage claim, I took her hand.

"I'm worried about you, SBB. That looked painful."

SBB closed her eyes and touched her pointer fingers to her temples. "No one understands the kind of pressure I am under."

"I'm trying to," I said. "But there's got to be a better way than eating anti-food according to a stopwatch."

"I just can't do it on my own," she said, looking up at me with fear in her big blue eyes. "Will you help me, Flan? Pleeeease?"

Before I could answer, she was gripping my arm and leaning in to whisper, "Flan, there's a model type staring at you from across carousel B. Eleven o'clock! He's what the Aussies call a *mate*."

"SBB," I said, trying to follow her eye toward the model type, "don't they just call all guys *mate* here?"

"Fine," she huffed. "He's what the Aussies call a drop-dead foxy mate. Are you over Jony yet? Because I think this one might do the trick."

My eyes landed on Three-Date Dave, who was smirking at me flirtily. He lifted his bag off the carousel, made the "I'll call you" motion with his hand, then disappeared into the crowd.

"Ohmigod," SBB squealed. "You better start talking fast."

I thought about how to sum up my last plane ride and the rest of the trip leading up to it. I put my arm around SBB's shoulder.

"To answer your questions, yes and yes. I am over Alex and I will help you unleash your inner gladiatrix."

SBB practically leapt into my arms. This was an old stunt with her, but one that I realized I was going to have to ask her to limit, at least until the gladiatrix training was over. Straining to hold her up, I wondered whether it mattered that I was fibbing. I didn't know a thing about weight training, and I didn't know if I really was over Alex. The only thing I did know was that maybe these two things were somehow intertwined. I'd tried all sorts of indulgences this week to mend my broken heart—maybe what I needed to do was just throw myself into something completely unrelated. Something that required hard work, determination, and—

"Oh, Flan!" SBB trilled. "You won't regret this! How about we start tomorrow, say, four-thirty a.m.? That way we'll beat the commuter traffic. I'll set my watch right now! Hey, I see your duffel over there! I've got an idea: Will you time me to see how long it takes me to haul it back over here one-handed?" SBB thrust the Prada pocket watch into my hands. "On your mark, get set, go!"

Oh boy. Was this a terrible idea?

*T*he next morning, at exactly four-thirty, SBB slammed her Prada pocket watch against the wall.

"Don't these things have snooze buttons?" she moaned in the darkness, her voice muffled by her pillow.

In the other twin bed across the room, I was just awake enough to be grateful that SBB also wanted to snooze a little longer. We were crashing at the giant sandstone party house Patch had rented right on Bondi Beach. But since he and Agnes were on their way back from a two-day reef dive, so far all we'd seen of them was the key left under the mat, complete with full instructions about how to use everything from the toilet to the light switches (classic Agnes), and the half-eaten pizza in the fridge with all the pepperonis picked off (classic Patch).

"Oh, the guilt," SBB murmured sleepily. "Please don't tell JR how much you're letting me slack off."

"You know," I said, my eyes still closed, "I'm actually looking out for you. Everyone knows if you don't get eight hours of sleep, you might as well kiss your workout goals good-bye."

"Ooh," she whispered, catching herself halfway through a ladylike snore. "You're so rational when you're sleepy."

The next thing I knew, Patch was standing over my bed, shaking my foot to wake me up. "G'day, jetsetter." He grinned. "Welcome to the land down unda. We've got a breakfast bonfire going on the beach. You guys gonna sleep all day or what?"

I looked at the clock. It was almost eleven o'clock. SBB was going to kill me!

"Bring in the rabid lions," SBB called out in her sleep, clearly dreaming about her *Gladiatrix* role.

"SBB," I said tentatively, climbing out of bed, "I have some bad news."

She blinked her eyes open. "There are rabid tigers, too?"

"Uh, I don't know about that, but we slept a little later than we meant to. It's—"

"*Over!*" she wailed after she grabbed her broken pocket watch from the floor. "It's all over. I can't afford a wasted day! I'll never get the part now!"

"What's she talking about?" Agnes asked, popping

her head in the door. She looked much tanner than she had last week in the city, but she seemed just as full of nervous energy as she had prevacation. Right now, she was literally twiddling her thumbs.

"SBB's training for a part and we overslept," I explained. "It's no big deal—we'll just find a way to amp up the workout."

Agnes raised her eyes at Patch. "Why don't you introduce them to your meathead friend out there?" She turned to SBB. "There's nothing Tommy loves more than talking about his fulfilling life of weightlifting."

"No. No. Absolutely not," SBB said, hopping out of bed to pace the room in her pajamas. As she ran toward the bathroom to brush her teeth, she called, "There's no time for socializing. I need to pump some serious iron."

"Did someone say 'pump some serious iron'?" a voice called from the hallway.

Then I heard the skidding sound of SBB in socks, sliding straight into the wall.

"I guess she met Tommy." Patch laughed, tugging my ponytail and leading me into the living room.

Sitting on the couch overlooking the pristine beach was the most muscular beach bum I had ever seen in my life. Tommy was flipping through a glossy magazine called *Mate's Best Weights* and slurping up a smoothie approximately the size of Noodles.

"If you're looking for workout advice," Patch said, pointing at his friend, "you've come to the right place."

SBB didn't waste any time. She crouched in front of Tommy on the couch and assumed a pose of such reverence, it reminded me of how Feb interacted with the guru.

"Teach me," she said to the mass of muscle.

Ten minutes later, we were dressed and sitting in front of the bonfire on the beach. "Okay, the first thing you do," Tommy said, "is start with a good Aussie brekkie. Some people like eggs. I never say no to a burger with the lot."

Our eyes grew wide as we watched Tommy flip a huge burger from the grill onto his plate. He loaded up his bun with lettuce, tomato, onion, pineapple(!), beets(!), a healthy squirt of mayonnaise, and hot sauce. Then, instead of taking a bite, he threw me for another loop by handing the plate over to SBB. "Now don't be shy if you want seconds," he said. "Flan, you want the lot too?"

As we munched on our Aussie-size breakfast burgers, which were actually shockingly delicious—the pineapple added just the right zing—SBB described in meticulous detail her training program to Tommy, and I flipped through *Mate's Best Weights*, dog-earing pages that I thought could offer SBB useful tips.

If you asked me a week ago which profession I'd be *least* likely to have, personal trainer might have sprung to mind. But working out in the fresh air on this silky, sandy beach, with the crystal water crashing right before our eyes—well, it didn't really seem like work at all. It was especially fun to feel like we had a whole team collaborating together. Agnes ran back and forth from the kitchen to the beach to make sure we were staying hydrated with her awesome lemon basil iced tea. Even Patch went down to the surf shop to bring back a few surfboards so we could use them as aerobic steps for beachside training.

Watching SBB and me do a set of crunches on the beach, he yawned, cracked open a soda, and said, "At this rate, you two are going to be the buffest chicks at the party tomorrow night."

"What party tomorrow night?" I asked, instantly giving up on the twenty-seven sit-ups I had left.

"Didn't I tell you we're throwing a barbecue—?"

"An *haute* barbecue," Agnes corrected.

"Whatever." Patch rolled his eyes. "Since you're only in town for a few days, Agnes and I wanted to throw you a party. To show you how it's done down under. A bunch of our friends will be there, so it's sure to get pretty wild."

I glanced at SBB. "Do you think we can take the night off training tomorrow to hit this party?"

She sighed and chewed on her lip. "Only if we really crack the workout whip during the day! And no sleeping in until eleven! And don't we have twenty-seven more sit-ups to do? Who's the drill sergeant here and who's the slacker? Huh?"

"Okay, okay," I said, lying back down in the sit-up position. "Twenty-seven, twenty-six!" I called out.

We pushed ourselves until late in the afternoon, staying super busy and super focused on Operation Beef It Up. In fact, the sun was starting to dip down toward the horizon when I realized: I hadn't thought of Alex all day. I'd been so busy—leading SBB though set after set of squats, calling her out when she didn't touch her nose to the sand during push ups, and making her jump rope for a minute every time she complained.

When I finally did think of Alex, it was because I stopped focusing on the starlet at hand to look out at an unusually large pelican fishing for its dinner. I knew Alex thought that pelicans were really underappreciated birds, especially the ones along the East

River, so the sight of one just sent me on a spiral of negative thoughts.

"What's wrong?" SBB asked, panting after a hundred-meter sprint. "Did you pull a muscle watching *me* work my butt off?"

"No," I said, looking down at my feet. "I just started thinking about Alex."

"But I thought you said yesterday—oh, Flan," she said, taking in my expression and hugging me. "I've been so selfish. Me and my superficial fitness goals. Do you want to talk about it?"

"No," I said quickly. "At this point, that's exactly what I *don't* want to do. I want what I said yesterday to be true. And your superficial fitness goals have been the best thing so far in terms of keeping my mind off him."

"Because Bianca—"

"I don't need Bianca," I insisted, mentally crossing my fingers that this was true. "I need—"

Just then, my phone started to ring. It was the ringtone for 'unknown number,' and SBB grabbed it off the beach towel. "I think it's an Aussie number," she said.

It didn't occur to me that the only Aussie with my number was Three-Date Dave until I'd already picked up.

"Hello?" I said.

"So I'm feeling a lot of pressure to plan really something special for our fourth date," he said with his adorable accent. Even over the phone, I could hear the smile in his voice. "What are you doing tomorrow night?"

"Oh—my brother's throwing a party," I said, feeling a little let down that my time in Oz was already so booked.

"Hmm," Dave said. "Well there goes all my hard work planning. I've an idea. What if you bailed on the party so I could take you night scuba diving? Parties come and go, right?"

I hesitated. Dave was being pretty forward, and I still didn't know him that well. Even though scuba diving sounded awesome, I really did want to go to this party.

"Well, it's kind of in my honor, so I need to at least make a cameo," I said, then I felt SBB's smack on my arm. "Ow . . . I mean . . . you should come to the party. It's going to be a barbecue—"

"*Haute* barbecue!" Agnes yelled from the porch to correct me.

"Er, haute barbecue," I corrected myself. "It's no scuba diving, but if my brother's track record says anything, it'll still be a blast."

"If you're there," Dave said, "I'm there. See you tomorrow night.'

When I hung up the phone, I could feel a grin spreading across my face.

"*Well?*" SBB demanded.

I turned to my gladiatrix friend and shrugged. "Looks like Three-Date Dave is on his way to lucky number four."

$\mathcal{E}$arly Saturday morning, the shrill sound of a whistle blowing pierced the tranquil Aussie air. When I opened my eyes, I could tell it was barely dawn. So what was SBB already doing out of bed? And who was that broad-shouldered blond gorilla hovering in our doorway?

"You have eight minutes to get dressed, get hydrated, and meet me at station one," the stranger barked, the whistle still stuck between her lips.

"Ten four, Jo!" SBB chirped, sounding much more awake than I thought she had a right to pre-sunrise. "Can I bring my friend Flan? She's my moral support."

Jo ran her cold beady eyes over me and said, "She either works it or you leave her at home. I have no patience for lollygaggers." She glanced down at her stopwatch before turning to walk down the dark hallway. "I'll see you in seven and a half minutes," she commanded over her shoulder.

"Yikes," I whispered to SBB. "I never knew an Australian accent could sound so scary. I thought these people were supposed to be laid-back."

"Shhhh!" SBB hissed. "She'll hear you! Its very important to start training with a blank slate."

"SBB, what is going on?" I said, finally sitting up and rubbing my eyes.

"Promise you won't be mad," she said, sitting down at the foot of my bed and whipping her blond hair into a high ponytail. "Last night, Tommy suggested that if I really wanted to get serious, I needed to call in a dedicated specialist. He gave me Jo's number." She lowered her voice to a whisper. "She's the only female rugby coach in the history of the South Sydney league."

She held up a navy blue rugby jersey, then pointed to the cursive team name, *Rabbitohs*, printed across the chest.

"See?" she said, pulling it over her head.

The jersey was kind of cool, but it was also at least six sizes too big for her.

"What happened to all the cute workout clothes you bought at Saks last week?"

SBB looked up from the leggings she was tugging

on. "Duh," she said, sounding bewildered. "I burned them."

"What?" I gasped. "Why?"

"I mean, I didn't literally burn them—I donated them to the Aerobics Instructors for Change campaign, but Flan, those clothes are dead to me. I bought them on Black Thursday—the day you know who"—she pointed at me—"found out about you know what." She mimed a broken heart. "Solidarity, Flan. I would never wear those clothes in front of you."

I shook my head, still processing her idea of solidarity. "That's really sweet, SBB, but you didn't have to do that. Those clothes don't have anything to do with . . ." I trailed off. "I wouldn't have taken it personally if you wore them."

SBB hugged me. "Then you won't take it personally that I outsourced a personal trainer? It doesn't mean I don't think you were dedicated to the cause. I just need someone to scare me into buffness, and rumor has it Jo's an absolute terror."

I shook my head and laughed, secretly relieved that this terror was going to take some of the pressure off of me. "I'm glad you found her. But are you sure you want to put yourself through this?"

SBB stood up, took a deep breath, and nodded.

"I'm sure," she said, "but it'd be a whole lot easier if . . ."

Timidly, she bent down to grab something from a shopping bag. When she held it up, I could see that it was a second, slightly larger Rabbitohs jersey, and another pair of gray leggings to match the ones she'd pulled on. She held them out toward me.

"Okay," I said, pulling the jersey over my head. "Solidarity."

"YOU'RE LATE!" Jo's shrill voice echoed through the house.

SBB and I scrambled into the kitchen, grabbed two of Agnes's homemade raisin bran muffins from the counter on our way out the door, and dashed outside in search of station one.

As we approached, Jo's wide-set eyes sized us up, as if she were taking note of our jogging form. Was it a bad sign that I already had a cramp? Jo did look every bit the terror, with her fierce black strip of zinc oxide down her nose and under both her eyes. She was standing in front of a pale yellow cone-shaped structure that extended at least thirty feet into the air.

"Behold," she said, "the Challenge Cheese."

When I stepped closer and could make out the toeholes scattered across the rubber cone, it really did look a lot like a giant wedge of Swiss cheese.

"Rule number one," Jo yelled, hands on her hips. "What did I say about lollygaggers? Rule number two," she continued without pausing. "Don't talk at all, ever, all day. No apologizing. No excuses. No complaints. *No words*. Get it?"

"Yes, Jo—"

"NO WORDS!" she bellowed. "Now climb up and down the Challenge Cheese until I tell you to stop."

SBB and I had time to shoot each other one terrified glance before Jo's "FASTER!" propelled us into motion. We clambered up either side of the challenge cone, pausing only to smile at each other sympathetically when we reached the top. Every time we got back down to the bottom, Jo would blow her whistle to send us back up again. My arms and my butt were killing me after the third time up the cone, and I could tell SBB was straining too.

"I am *so* out of shape," I whispered the next time we both reached the top.

"Before this week, the last time I worked out, Bendel's was still carrying fur!" SBB commiserated quickly, before jetting back down the cheese cone.

Before I could even crack up, Jo laid right on her whistle.

"What part of NO WORDS do you two pansies not understand? Do I have to take you to the Suicide

Slide to shut you up?" she barked. "Station number two. NOW!"

The Suicide Slide at station two was even more of a butt-cruncher than the cone. And the Death by Ropes course at station three totally killed my abs. By the time we'd been through all eight stations, SBB and I could hardly breathe, and we definitely couldn't walk.

"Please tell me I'm going to wake up a gladiatrix," SBB moaned, collapsing on the sand.

"Actually, you're going to wake up quite sore," Jo said, in a much softer, much more human voice. "Here," she said, holding out a cupped hand to SBB. "Aspirin and aloe water. The world's greatest muscle-mending cocktail. You too, Flan—drink up."

"Am I hallucinating?" SBB said, turning to me. "Or did Jo just say something moderately nice to us?"

"Only *moderately* nice, am I?" Jo laughed, taking a seat on the beach between us. She unzipped a backpack and pulled out a few Tupperware containers, opening them up and offering us a selection of tropical fruit, whole wheat crackers, and cheddar cheese. SBB and I watched in silent awe.

"Since you only hired me for the day, I can let you guys in on my little secret." She shrugged. "I'm actually an incredibly nice person. The coarse façade is

just my work face, when I need to get the job done."
For a second her tone shifted back to the old Jo as she
threatened, "But don't you dare tell any of the rugby
mates that—or else all of Australia will blame you for
a losing season."

SBB nearly choked on her chunk of cheddar
cheese. "Can I just say, when I become a member of
the Academy, I will totally give you an Oscar for your
performance today. How did you *do* that?"

Jo stood up and moved behind SBB to start mas-
saging her tense shoulders. "I've seen your movies,
Sara Beth. You do the same thing yourself. We all do."
She turned to me. "Right, Flan?"

The first thing that shot into my head was the
façade I was putting up in front of SBB so she
wouldn't know that I was still feeling really down
about the breakup. Obviously that was not something
to bring up in present company, so I just stammered
something like, "Oh, I'm not a very good actress."

"Ha!" SBB laughed. "That's the understatement of
the millennium. Flan has the worst poker face ever.
You can always tell exactly what she's thinking." She
patted my knee. "But it's one of her most endearing
qualities."

When I looked up at SBB, I couldn't figure out
whether it was a good thing or a bad thing that she

didn't know how badly I was hurting. Sometimes I thought it would feel so good just to vent to her, but then, I didn't want to distract her from her training. And also, who was I kidding? I was terrified of the wrath of Bianca. I wondered if there was any chance that Bianca would turn out to be like Jo—with just a tough exterior to get the job done.

"Speaking of bad poker faces," Jo chimed in, "neither one of you can fool me that you're totally and completely wiped out. The buzz is that there's a big party tonight in your honor." She smiled, then turned back on the drill sergeant one last time. "Now get home and recharge for at least three hours. That's an order!"

*I*t looks so harmless now, doesn't it?" SBB asked later that evening. We were standing on the deck, watching the sun set over the very same beach where Jo had kicked our butts just a few hours earlier. Since then, we'd spent the mandated three recharging hours washing the sand out of our hair and sleeping off some of the exhaustion. But even though we'd cleaned up pretty well in our patterned silk maxidresses, the training pain was still very fresh in both our minds.

"I'm never going to look at Swiss cheese the same way again," I agreed, slurping down my third aloe water of the day.

"Ouch, I know—just thinking about it sends a shooting pain down my glutes." SBB winced, reaching around to massage her muscles. "Oh my God, do I have buns of steel or do I have buns of steel?" She grabbed my hand to make me cop a feel.

I laughed. "Jo might be a terror, but she delivers results. Those are the most gladiatrixed-out buns I've ever felt."

"Maybe you need a second opinion on that?" a guy's voice asked from behind us. It was Dave, looking amazing in a pristine white linen shirt and faded jeans. His look was a far cry from that of most of the posh city boys we usually ran with, but SBB shot me an approving thumbs-up.

I stepped toward him to give him a hug. "I thought you were going to meet us at the party," I said.

"I thought you two could use an escort." He shrugged.

At that moment, I realized that I actually had no idea how to get to the party. Patch had said something about a pier at the north end of Bondi, but he was never very good with directions.

"I was told it's just a couple miles down the beach," Dave said, reading my mind and pointing north.

Just a couple of miles? SBB and I exchanged a worried look. It was hard enough to walk on the beach in kitten heels when you *hadn't* spent six hours working your legs to the consistency of Jell-O.

Dave cleared his throat. "I hope it's okay that I brought a few friends. They know the way a little bit better than I do."

Following his finger with my eyes, I expected to see a few other guys on the beach, but Dave was pointing at a palm tree on the other side of the deck. I squinted to make out three white horses tethered to it with a rope. "Shall we?"

Being fashionably late in New York means showing up twenty minutes after the invitation time with a box of Fat Witch brownies and a Diane von Furstenberg dress that no one else is wearing.

Being fashionably late in Sydney means arriving half an hour late because you decided to take your gleaming white horse for a little bit longer of a beach-front joyride. The Diane von Furstenberg dress that no one else was wearing didn't hurt either. And having a boy as cute as Dave lead us in made up for the fact that I couldn't get my hands on any of Manhattan's favorite brownies.

The "haute" barbecue was being held on a wide pier overlooking the cliffs of Ramsgate Point. A band was playing chilled-out reggae versions of Beatles songs, and a bunch of beach chic–clad partygoers were already dancing on blankets spread out around the sand. The sun was just hitting the water on the horizon when we walked through the line of tiki torches to be greeted by waiters serving oyster shooters off adorable mini surfboards.

"Killer party, Patch," I called to my brother, who was manning the grill at the edge of the pier.

"Hey, Flan." He waved his tongs at me. "*Haute* dog?"

I guessed he'd put his foot down despite Agnes's arguments that *haute* meant catered. SBB and I grabbed a couple hot dogs and sat down on a picnic table to watch Agnes angrily multitask—arranging a cluster of red gladiolas in a vase while berating Tommy for showing up in just a bathing suit. When SBB and I stepped past them to find a spot with less drama, Agnes was yelling, "No shirt, no shoes, no haute barbecue!"

Aside from the BBQzilla, the party seemed like a total success. After dinner, we nibbled on caramelized banana skewers and slurped virgin piña coladas out of coconut shells. SBB and I made a cameo appearance on the dance floor for the limbo, even though the aftermath of the day's workout caused us both to get eliminated in the first round. But it was still so fun to watch Danny, Patch, and Tommy all hang on until the very last round. Looking around the beach, it was amazing to be halfway around the world, but still be at a party that felt so much like home.

When SBB went up to the band to request that

they play some Jake Riverdale songs, I felt a tap on my shoulder.

"There you are," a soft voice said. I turned around to see Jo, who gave me a quick hug. I had to will myself not to clam up—I still wasn't used to not being terrified of her.

"I want to introduce you to someone," she said. "But she's a new client, so I'm going to have to act tough, okay?"

"Sure," I said, surprised but a little flattered that Jo was seeking me out to meet one of her clients.

"You'll love this girl," Jo said as we walked back over toward the grill. "She's from Manhattan and she reminds me a lot of you." She paused behind a thin blond girl with her back to us.

"Ahem," Jo said, leaning over to tap her on the shoulder. "This client actually *succeeded* at my work-out. Try to take a lesson from her."

The girl turned around slowly, flipping her blond hair out of her eyes to smile.

"Flan Flood," Jo said, "this is Cookie Monsoon."

Cookie Monsoon was standing in front of me, nibbling on a banana skewer that my own flesh and blood had grilled, wearing an Alexander McQueen maxi that was too close for comfort to my own DVF. Oh. My. God.

"Nice to meet you," she said in a supersweet voice. When she smiled, it was like someone had taken a hatchet to my chest. "I started training today for the New York triathlon, and Jo just about killed me. What are you, Wonder Woman?"

I shook my head, still stunned.

Then she leaned in to whisper in my ear—Cookie Freaking Monsoon was whispering in my ear! "Is it just me, or does Jo act scarier than she needs to?"

Was this wrecking ball of a human being actually trying to confide in me? I guessed this party didn't need Fat Witch brownies. Here was the fattest witch in the world—except she wasn't acting like a witch at all, and she was actually really pretty and cute. Who did she think she was? And how dare she act like she didn't know who *I* was?

Oh, wait—what if she *didn't* know who I was? What if Alex hadn't even mentioned me at all?

Immediately, I started sniffing around for him. Of course he'd be spending spring break with this . . . replacement. Had Camille's text about the Knicks game been a total lie?

I knew Cookie was staring at me, waiting for a response, but I was too stunned even to open my mouth.

"So, where do you live in the city?" she filled in

after a pause. "I'm in the West Village, on Jane Street, but I go to school up at Spence, so I have to hustle all the way uptown every day. It's kind of a drag."

Why wouldn't she shut up? Why did she just keep talking so that every word she said felt like a nail in my coffin?

"What brings you to Australia?" she blabbered on cruelly. "I'm visiting my—"

"Um, I have to go. 'Bye," I blurted, then turned and ran as quickly as I could, as far away from Cookie as possible.

I was gasping for breath by the time I reached the water. The tide was super low, perfectly matching my spirits. My legs throbbed. My heart ached. I collapsed in a heap on a rock, realizing with a sniff that I'd bolted so quickly out of the party, I'd left my bag inside. I didn't even have my phone to SOS text SBB. And there was no way I was going back in there.

"Flan? Is that you?" I looked up to see Dave, who looked concerned, but whom I really didn't want to see right now. "What happened?"

I shook my head. I couldn't talk. I tried to mentally will Dave to go away, but instead he sat down and put his arm around me. We sat like that for a minute, with him just holding my shaking shoulders. Then, without warning, I felt his hands on my face and his big lips on mine. It was all, *all* wrong.

"No." I pulled away quickly. "I don't want to. I can't."

"You need to forget about that other guy," Dave said firmly. "I can help you." He came back in for another kiss, this time starting out by shoving his tongue between my lips.

"Hey!" I leapt up. "I said no, I meant no."

"Whatever," he said, sounding annoyed, like I was the one acting inappropriate. "Your loss," he scoffed, throwing up his arms. He stood up. I didn't even look at him.

I could have ripped into him about how out of line he was, but I didn't even feel like wasting my breath. I was already so exhausted. When Dave stormed back toward the party, I sank back down on the rock, not even caring that my dress was getting ruined by seaweed and wet sand.

All I could think about was Alex and Cookie, Cookie and Alex. Tonight—scratch that, this whole week—had been absolute torture. I'd exhausted three continents and still, I had failed. It was the end of spring break—but I was still broken.

"resh-baked cookie?" the Manhattan-based flight attendant said, leaning over my seat and lifting up a cloth napkin to reveal a basket of warm chocolate chip cookies. My stomach turned as I caught a whiff of their straight-out-of-the-oven goodness. I pulled the hood of my gray Pleasure Principle T-shirt over my head and practiced disappearing.

"*No*," SBB commanded the flight attendant, pushing the basket away and covering my hooded ears with her hands. "Absolutely no *cookies*! Come to think of it, no desserts of any kind. Say, you don't happen to have any Energy Glide on this jet, do you? Wild berry flavor maybe?"

I sneaked a peek at the flight attendant, who was chewing her brightly lined lip. It might have been the first time any passenger had turned down her fresh-baked cookie offer.

"I can check in the back, sweetie," she said to SBB, before turning to the row behind us with her basket of cookies.

"Ohhhh," SBB said worriedly. "Why didn't I take JR's advice and pack a bigger supply of Energy Glide? I thought I needed the suitcase space for my Gryphon belted cape, which of course was totally wrong for the beach—"

I cleared my throat, preparing to speak for the first time all day, other than when the TSA security guy had asked me if I had any explosive materials in my carry-on.

"We'll be back in Manhattan in, ugh, fourteen hours. I'm sure you can get your Energy Glide fix there."

"Well, it can't come quickly enough," SBB said, fidgeting nervously.

My thoughts exactly. We'd been airborne for less than an hour, and I was already going stir-crazy. With nothing to do but stare out the window and listen to SBB yap on about her protein ratio, my mind couldn't stop running over all the awful details of last night.

"How much more muscle mass do you need for *Gladiatrix*?" I asked her, trying to shake up my mind's only subject, even though I was just about at the limit of my capacity for body-mass-index talk.

SBB made her hesitant lip-pursing face for a minute, then said, "Actually, I don't need the Energy Glide for weight gain anyway. I'm just a *little* bit addicted."

"What?" I said. "I thought that was the point of that nasty gel."

"It is," she said, looking down at the cut of her own biceps with an admiring glance. "Or anyway, it was. But . . . the truth is, Flan, I met my goal when I weighed in with Jo this morning."

"*What?*" I said, not sure whether I should smack her or hug her. "Why didn't you tell me? SBB, that's huge! Congratulations."

"Thanks," she said, reaching for the airline magazine in the seat pocket, pulling it out, and realizing that her face was on the cover. "Huh. Well, I guess I didn't mention it today because I know you're still recovering from last night. You've been having such a rough week, Flannie. I didn't it want to seem like I was rubbing it in that I met my goal."

I patted her massive quad. "That's really sweet, SBB. But seriously, you don't have to shield me from your success just because I'm having a hard time. I'm proud of you."

"Thanks," she said. "Now all I have to do is mass maintenance until the first read of the script next

week. Once Holly Hendrix—she's the casting director, total hater, one of those unmarried early thirties
types—anyway, once she sees the evidence of my
commitment," she said, flashing me another shot of
her biceps, "she'll have to eat her five-syllable words.
Hmph!"

"You'll show her," I said noncommittally. I could
feel myself starting to zone out of the conversation.
Maybe SBB could just talk me into some sort of
fourteen-hour-long trance. . . .

"And the best part is," she continued, unaware of
my waning interest, "Jo's agreed to help me. We're
going to webcam."

"I used to webcam with Alex," I said robotically,
remembering his smile when we'd first connect from
our respective computer labs at school. I was always
supposed to be doing my French oral practice, but
whenever I saw Alex's screen name—FFslaxguy—
online, it was impossible to resist IMing him. I
couldn't help wondering if he'd already changed his
screen name to something honoring Cookie.

SBB sighed. "See, there I go again, getting all
wrapped up in my training," she said, turning to me.
"Let's make the rest of this flight all about you. What
do *you* want to talk about? What do *you* want to do?"

"Disappear," I said, pulling my hood up again.

SBB flopped my hood back down a little bit more aggressively than she needed to. "Instead of that," she said, flipping to the back of the in-flight magazine. "What do you say we watch a movie?"

"I guess." I sighed. "But no romantic comedies. No tortured love story dramas. No kissing," I said petulantly.

"*Okaaaay*, do you allow human beings in the movies that make your list? Jeez, scratch that idea." She slid the magazine back into the seat. "I could show you a card trick. I learned a really impressive one from David Blaine when we were at the Magic Castle in L.A.—"

I groaned. "Card tricks make me think of Dave the Creeper—and I never want to think of him again."

"Motion denied," SBB said, scratching her chin. "And you probably don't want to meditate, because that will make you think of what a terrible time you had in Thailand, right?"

"Omigod," I said, slapping my forehead. "I just got an external glimpse of what an absolutely miserable person I've become. I can't believe this. I'm so negative. This isn't me. This is all Alex's fault. And Cookie's. And Kennedy's. And—"

"Okay," SBB interrupted. "Instead of pointing your pretty little fingers—though personally, I wouldn't mind sticking all of this on Kennedy—maybe what we need to do is turn off the pressure cooker." She mimicked turning a switch on the side of my head down low.

"It's not working." I sniffed.

"I'm starting to feel like this is all *my* fault, for only giving you a week to get over him. I shouldn't have put a timeline on your emotions." She put a hand to her chest. "I mean, what am I, a presidential nominee? Some day, maybe—Washington does love its actors, you know?"

I shrugged.

"What I'm saying, Flannie, is you're just going to have to heal on your own time. So your sadness spills outside of spring break." She gave a Woody Allen shrug. "Who cares? Whenever you do get over it—"

"If I get over it," I butted in.

"*When* you get over it, I will throw you a party so fantastic you'll forget we ever even had this silly argument."

"I hope you're right." I sighed.

"Of course I'm right," SBB said, flexing her pecs and her delts and her triceps and some other muscle group near her neck that I never even knew existed. "Do I need to use force to get you to tell me what I want to hear?"

"Okay, okay—you win," I made myself say. "I *will* get over this, and when I do, you *will* throw me a party."

"A *fantastic* party," she corrected.

"A fantastic party. Jeez, I can't wait until you get this part so you can start taking your energy out in the gladiator pit instead of on me."

SBB grinned and snuggled her head into my shoulder. "From your mouth to Holly Hendrix's ears."

*H*ey Flan!" a chipper voice greeted me Sunday evening when I went to pick Noodles up from the Village Kennel Club. It was Pam Austin, the owner of the kennel, and possibly Noodles's second biggest fan in the world.

"Hi Pam," I said, stepping over the series of doggie gates to get to the front desk. But Pam didn't hear me; she'd already ducked into the back room to grab Noodles. For a place that housed up to twenty dogs at a time, Village Kennel Club always managed to smell like cinnamon and vanilla. "Thanks for bending the rules for me," I called to Pam.

My flight from Sydney hadn't landed until seven, and usually the Kennel Club was closed for pickups after six on Sundays, but Pam had agreed in advance to let me pick Noodles up as soon as I got back to the city. I was especially grateful now, seeing as how SBB had taken a connecting flight from JFK to Montreal to see JR. And my whole family was still in the three other corners of the world. And none of my Thoney friends would even land from their Paris flight until almost midnight tonight.

I really didn't want to have to go home to an empty house, but I figured, armed with Noodles, my dark foyer would be a little bit easier to handle.

"Here he is, Mr. Noodley Noo!" Pam sang in her dog voice. She appeared back behind the front desk with my happy, squirming Pomeranian in her hands. She held him out to me, and when I lifted him to my chest to give him a hug, my heart swelled with love. Noodles showered me with such a forceful slew of kisses, I had to sit down.

"Ooh," I said, taking in his freshly bathed fur. "A new blue collar. That's a good color for you, Noods."

"Well, I have to tell you," Pam said, leaning over the desk conspiratorially, "it's not just the collar making him look so good. While you were off gallivanting all over the globe, Noodles had a very busy week himself."

"What do you mean?" I asked. He looked like the same old guy to me.

"Let's just say he unleashed his inner Romeo." She nodded. "That's right. Your Noodles fell in love."

I gave Pam a bewildered look. Not because Noodles wasn't lovable—he was! But because with everything else this week . . . it was just such ridiculous timing.

"Frances will be very sad to see him go." Pam said. "Do you want to meet her?"

"Oh," I said. "I hadn't really thought about it, but . . . okay. Sure." When Pam disappeared into the kennel a second time, I turned to Noodles. "You fell in love with a dog named Frances? Who is this girl?"

At the sound of the tinkle of tags coming from the back, Noodles's ears perked to attention. He barked once, hopped right off my lap, and went to wait by the back door, tail flying back and forth. The only time I'd never seen him act like this was when we had leftover pizza from John's.

Pam opened the door and a fat little pug with gray whiskers and a pink bow around her neck waddled right up to Noodles. She snorted and sneezed and wagged her own crooked curly tail in a circle while Noodles showered her with kisses, making me feel slightly less special. Of course, I wanted to be happy for Noodles, but did he really have to pick this week to fall in love?

"It's always hard when they have to part ways after making such a connection," Pam whispered. I knew she was a pretty eccentric dog lover, but she actually sounded like she might cry right then. Was her lip really quivering? "If you want, I could put you in touch with Frances's owner. Maybe"—she paused dramatically—"this doesn't have to be good-bye."

"Sure," I said, looking down at Noodles. He did look like he'd want to keep in touch with his lady pug. While Pam looked up Frances's owner's contact information on the computer, I had a momentary fantasy about whom she might belong to. What if it was a tall, dark, handsome, and eternally faithful guy who just happened to be single and attracted to girls with just a smidge of baggage? SBB *had* just been telling me to try to see the silver lining in this situation. It could happen, right?

"Here we go," Pam said, taking out a piece of paper to make a note. "Doris Westerlake of West Eighth Street. Not too far away. Here's her number. When she gets back from her hip-replacement surgery, I'll let her know you might be in touch."

Hmm, it sounded like Doris Westerlake was not going to be the next great love of my life. It also sounded like I was getting a little delirious. I needed to take Noodles and go home.

"Say good-bye to Frances, Noodles," I cooed. "Maybe you'll see her again."

On the short walk back to our brownstone, Noodles was decidedly downtrodden. I'd thought I'd wanted him to give my own spirits a boost, but it was actually kind of nice to wallow in our loneliness together.

"What would you say to an order of lo mein from Tang's and a big long snuggle on the couch?" I asked him. He wagged his tail in response. Neither one of us ever said no to lo mein.

I opened the front door and set Noodles down to give him free sniffing rein in the hallway, then went to check the mail from the overflowing box on our front stoop. I took the massive stack inside and plopped down on the couch to sort through it. Mom's spa catalogues . . . Dad's golf and wine magazine subscriptions . . . two boxes of weird earthy products Feb had ordered online . . . and Patch's Princeton newsletter.

And ooh—a nice stack of Frenchie postcards from the girls. Maybe this would tide me over until we all reconvened tomorrow morning.

With Noodles curled in my lap and the call put into Tang's for lo mein delivery, I started to go through them.

The first was a black-and-white picture of a mustached French man standing along the Seine, smoking a cigarette and wearing a beret. On the back, Amory had written:

ALL THE FRENCH BOYS LOOK LIKE THIS DUDE—YOU TOTALLY LUCKED OUT GOING TO ITALY! CAN'T WAIT TO SWAP STORIES WITH YOU. XX—A

The second was a print of one of Monet's water lily paintings, and on the back was Harper's note:

MUSÉE D'ORSAY IS *FANTASTIQUE*. BUT IT WASN'T HALF AS GOOD AS IT WOULD HAVE BEEN WITH YOU BY OUR SIDES. HOPE YOUR WEEK WAS AS TRANQUIL AS THESE WATER LILIES. WE MISS YOU! LOVE, HARP

The third was from Morgan, the history buff. It was a photograph of an aerial view from the top of the Arc de Triomphe on the Champs-Elysées:

IF PARIS REBUILT ITSELF AFTER WORLD WAR TWO AND HAS THIS MONUMENT TO PROVE IT—YOU CAN TOO! ANYTIME YOU NEED A BOY BOYCOTT, JUST SAY THE WORD. HANG IN THERE! LOVE, MORG

When I got to the fourth postcard, I knew it would be from Camille. It was another black-and-white photo of two elderly French ladies sitting at an outdoor café and gossiping. I flipped it over:

THIS IS RIDICULOUS. I CAN'T BELIEVE I'M HERE AND YOU'RE NOT. LET'S NEVER SPEND SPRING BREAK APART AGAIN. LET'S BE THESE TWO OLD BIRDS, LAUGHING LIKE LUNATICS SIDE BY SIDE FROM HERE ON OUT. LOVE YOU, C

Underneath Camille's really heartwarming post-card, there was a fifth and final postcard. Had the girls all written me one together? Was that the Luxembourg Gardens? Why did it look so much like Central Park? I flipped it over:

FLAN,

I STAYED IN THE CITY THIS WEEK. I FOUND THIS POST-CARD IN A LIBRARY BOOK I CHECKED OUT. AT LEAST THERE'VE BEEN SOME GOOD BASKETBALL GAMES TO WATCH.

ALEX

Alex? Was this some kind of joke? Or some sort of hate letter in secret code? I didn't get it. If he was just going to send a cryptic postcard, why had he bothered to write at all? My hands were shaking. What was he trying to do to me?

Chapter 21
THE PROBLEM WITH THE POSTCARD

*S*ince late March in Manhattan often meant late-season snowfall, my friends and I had agreed to forgo our normal meeting spot on the front steps of the Met and convene Monday morning in the Thoney freshman lounge for hot chocolate and even hotter debriefing.

I arrived early, to give myself some time to figure out how to position The Postcard Incident. I was doling out mini-marshmallow cocoa toppings when the girls burst through the door.

"Oh my God!! There she is!"

It was the best kind of ambush: all my Thoney girls, dressed to *les neufs*, running full throttle toward me. I dropped the bag of marshmallows, and the girls and I flung our arms around each other, resulting in the most convoluted, tangled group hug our school had ever seen. Morgan actually tumbled over from the excitement of the heap and almost knocked over the Fiji water cooler.

"We missed you sooooooooo much!" the girls all shouted.

"Tell us all about Italy!" Harper breathed.

"And Thailand!" Amory said, squeezing my hand.

"And Sydney," Morgan said, shaking her head in disbelief.

"Seriously," Camille said. "I know your family is a walking travelogue, but you bring new meaning to the word *Flood*."

"It was a crazy week," I acknowledged. "But I missed you guys so much. You have to tell me all about the GPA ASAP."

"You mean *l'aventure Parisian d'or*?" Amory said, in a pitch-perfect Parisian French accent.

"*Oui, oui, bien sûr!*" I grinned, taking in her ombre-washed mauve jeans. "Love these pants! Are they Jade Moodswings?"

Amory shook her head. "Zadig & Voltaire, my new favorite store. But Harper's getup is a Moodswing orig. It's from the new line, Sophistiqué."

Harper spun around to show off her navy blue sheath dress topped with a pea green cardigan with a peacock-feather neckline. *Sophistiqué* it was.

Amory turned to whisper conspiratorially to Camille, "Should we do it now or later?"

"As if we could wait another second." Camille laughed, pulling out a huge crepe paper–wrapped package out from her metallic leather Dior satchel. "Speaking of Moodswing originals . . ." She grinned, shoving it into my hands. "We brought you *un petit souvenir*. Okay, it's *un grand souvenir*."

"And since Jade already had your measurements," Morgan added, "it's totally couture. You'd better love it!"

I held the package in my hands, feeling out its magic. Whenever I unveiled a Jade Moodswing outfit, it always felt like Christmas morning. But as I looked around the lounge at all my friends' expectant faces, this particular unveiling felt even more special. It was tangible proof that I had some really amazing friends at Thoney.

A lot of cliques might have felt like they had to tiptoe around the juicy details of a trip that one of them had missed. But we weren't the type to waste any time on awkwardness. Especially when there were stories to be swapped and couture to be unwrapped.

"You guys!" I practically screamed when the last piece of wrapping paper fell away to expose a glittering red cocktail dress.

It was a tea-length, strapless, fluffy-skirted gown with gold embroidered poppies under a sheath of gauzy red silk. I'd never in my life seen anything so exotic—and after this week, that was saying a lot.

"This is unbelievable," I breathed.

"It'll be even more unbelievable," Camille said, holding it up to me, "on you!"

Looking down, I was instantly and completely obsessed with the dress, but somehow it didn't match up with my perception of Jade's couture. Come to think of it, neither did Harper's outfit. I loved them both, but it was kind of weird not to recognize the new sophisticated style of my very favorite designer. Had that much changed in fashion in the month since I'd last seen Jade?

"Is she still doing the urban grit line?" I asked, and immediately all the girls shook their heads.

"No, she's sort of moving into a space that's more glam than grit," Harper said seriously. "You *have* to see what she did with her atelier," she gushed, smoothing out the already perfectly positioned peacock feathers on her cardigan.

I nodded, but wondered when I was going to have the chance to do that—and how many trends would have come and gone by then.

"Luckily, Morgan took about a thousand pictures

so you'd be able to see it from every angle." Camille laughed.

I turned to my fellow photo-savvy friend and realized I was breathing a sigh of relief. "Really, you took pictures for me?"

"*Took* pictures doesn't exactly cover it." Morgan laughed. "Bennett got so annoyed with my camera obsession, he threatened to glue it to my face if I didn't put it away for at least one course of a meal." She started cracking up. "But I wanted you to be able to see everything. We found that fondue place in Montmartre that you'd listed in the GPA binder. Did you know they serve all the drinks in baby bottles?"

"As if the boys needed another excuse to act like infants," Harper joked.

Morgan winked at me. "I'll hook you up. I already have plans for a whole Flan-specific slide show, complete with sound track. It'll be like you never missed a thing."

I looked down at my feet and things got quiet for a moment. So maybe we *were* having the requisite awkward moment. I really was glad the girls had had such an amazing trip, and I loved, loved, loved my dress, but there was no getting around the fact that I *had* missed a thing. I'd missed a lot of things.

"Who wants cocoa?" Camille triaged, filling our

cups with hot milk and stirring the cocoa in. "An extrarich one with double marshmallows for Ms. Flood, who will proceed to tell us all about her tri-continental extravaganza."

· My friends all huddled around the table, grabbing seats and mugs of hot chocolate. They looked up at me with expectant faces.

"Well," I began, wondering how in the world my week could compete with theirs, "Sorrento was really pretty. Basically Mom and Dad spoiled me with cheese and ice cream for three solid days. Then I went to Thailand to visit Feb and had this really enlightening experience with a guru. Then I hung out in Sydney to help SBB with this movie she's making."

The girls waited.

"That's it?" Morgan finally asked.

"Ice cream? Guru? New SBB flick?? Details!!" Amory begged.

"Well, I also got this postcard from Alex," I said, reaching into my bag. "The truth is, I have no idea what to make of it. I can't get it out of my head."

The girls exchanged knowing looks.

"Okay," Camille said. "Let's have it."

I held up the image side of the postcard and swung it around the table for their perusal, exhibit-A style.

"Central Park." Amory nodded. "Civil and yet nonspecific."

Then I plunked the postcard on the table so my friends could read Alex's frustratingly cryptic message.

They read and reread, bit their lips, and scratched their heads. Amory slurped up a marshmallow.

"Who cares about basketball games?" Morgan said finally, breaking the silence.

"I *know*," Camille sounded appalled. "And what is up with this library book reference?"

"So it's not just me?" I asked. "He's being weird?"

"*So* weird," they all agreed, bobbing their heads.

"Look, Flan," Camille said, pulling her hair out of its bun, then putting it back up—her sign that she was not just collecting her hair but also her thoughts. "I should tell you something. Xander told me Alex was pretty miserable over spring break."

"But that doesn't make sense," I said. "You kept telling me he was at the Knicks game, and—"

"Yeah but just because he physically existed in places doesn't mean he was *happy*. You were in freaking Bangkok and I can tell from your face that you hated every second," she said, poking my side. "Yeah, we know you. You suck at the poker face. Look, we didn't tell you sooner because we all thought you needed time and space away from the situation. Right, girls?"

My friends nodded gravely.

"We didn't want to pull you back into the emotional turmoil while you were on your getaway." Camille shrugged. "But now that you've had some space, maybe you'll both be ready for some closure."

"I don't know," I said.

"Look, he can't just cheat on you, then send you weird postcards and expect it to be okay," Morgan huffed.

"Exactly," Amory said. "You need to call him out on this stuff and then put an end to the *communicado*."

"It's the only way you're going to make any progress," Harper agreed.

"But," I asked, "am I ready to see him?"

"Short and sweet, Flan," Morgan coached. "Like ripping off a Band-Aid. And if at any time you need a boy boycott—" she said.

"I know." I cut her off. "I know where to find you guys. Hopefully it won't come to that," I said.

The bell rang and we all looked at our watches, slurping up the last of our hot chocolate. I knew my friends were thinking that we had to book it to first period in under two minutes, but all I could think was that in under eight hours, I was going to have to reach out to Alex. I was going to have to take the Jerk of New York to task.

Chapter 22

*W*hen Alex agreed to meet me after school at our normal spot in the park, I had an unsettling bout of déjà vu. I always texted him right after lunch, and he always got back to me right before his lacrosse practice. Now I know people always say you can't read tone of voice into a text message, but those people probably never had their hearts trampled. The textual tension between us was palpable.

I don't know why I took the train down to the Fifty-ninth Street entrance only to walk back up to our meeting spot near Sixty-eighth. Maybe because I knew that, coming from Dalton, Alex might also go in through the Sixty-eighth Street entrance and we might unexpectedly meet up before the meeting place. Awkward.

I didn't want to think I'd gone all the way down there because I was sappy enough to want to pass our favorite hot dog vendor once more, for old time's sake. Not that I'd ever be able to eat a hot dog again without thinking about what a pig Alex was . . .

"Two hot dogs, extra relish." A guy was ordering from Hank, the hot dog vendor. Hey, that was *our* old order! And hey, that was my ex-boyfriend! Why did he have to look so amazing in his green Tod's turtleneck and frayed Diesel jeans? Why was his hair that perfect length exactly two weeks into his monthly haircut? Why was he ordering *two* hot dogs?

"Work up an appetite at lacrosse?" I asked, a bit more icily than I'd meant to. It was the first real exchange we'd had since the breakup, and I was not setting the civility bar very high.

"Flan!" He swung around to face me. His eyes were puppy dog wide. "I didn't, I wasn't . . . Itwasforyou," he finally blurted. "Dumb idea. Unless you want it . . . "

He held out the hot dog like it was some sort of weird, relish-covered white flag. I didn't want it, but I wasn't sure what to say. Would Alex think it was rude if I denied him? *Just take the hot dog, Flan.*

Instead of walking ten blocks north up to our favorite spot (for its view of Manhattan's only red-tailed hawk), both of us silently plunked down on the nearest bench. It was clear that we were both eager to get this over with. But it was also clear that neither one of us knew where to start. We sat facing the street, watching the city go by. There was the woman getting splashed by a bus driving through the winter sludge. There was the dog walker chasing after three miniature poodles who'd gotten loose outside the Plaza. There were the cabs cutting each other off to get one car ahead in gridlock. And there was the unhappy couple (us) finishing off the breakup. Sometimes Manhattan could be so cruel.

"So, how was spring break?" Alex finally broke the silence. "I heard you were in Australia?"

I whipped my head to look at him. He heard? Had Cookie already told him about the awful scene at the haute barbecue?

"The guys, you know, they texted me from Paris," he went on. "It wasn't like I was stalking you or anything—I just meant, it sounds like you had a lot of fun."

I looked at Alex like he'd just implied that the ninth circle of hell was probably a lot of fun too. Ugh, this fake small talk had to end.

"Actually, my spring break sucked," I said bluntly. "I couldn't get a certain picture out of my head."

"What picture?" He squinted at me.

OMG, was he really going to make me spell it out for him?

"The picture," I exclaimed, "of you kissing Cookie Monsoon!"

That was when Alex spit out his mouthful of hot dog, sending the relish-filled bite directly into a lucky pigeon's path. "Excuse me?" he said. "Kissing what? I have no idea what you're talking about."

I rolled my eyes. "I almost deleted this when Kennedy evilly forwarded it to me last week to rub it in as much as possible," I said, reaching into my coat pocket for my iPhone. "But if this is what it takes to get you to admit it . . ."

I pulled up the infamous picture and shoved it under Alex's nose with the same vengeance with which Kennedy had shoved it under mine last week. Alex brought it closer to his face, squinted, then started laughing.

"This is funny to you?" I huffed.

"It's so unfunny," he said, cropping the photo to zoom in. "*Kennedy* sent this to you? Kennedy, your sworn enemy?"

"So what?" I said, crossing my arms and hating that he was making me defend her. "A picture is worth a thousand bitchy words."

"Flan, I don't even know who this girl in the picture is. She looks vaguely familiar, in that we-were-at-the-same-party-as-two-hundred-other-people kind of way. But I didn't even talk to her that night, let alone kiss her, as this—excuse me—very, very poorly doctored photo might suggest."

"What?" I gasped, grabbing the phone. "Doctored photo?"

Alex nodded. "Clearly whoever's behind this never took Photoshop 101 with Mr. Keys at Dalton. Exhibit A—the entire leg and arm of the person sitting in between me and this girl." He pointed at the screen. "I was sitting next to my lacrosse buddy, Dane, the entire night and that, right there, is his varsity championship ring."

Whoa. There *was* a phantom hand and kneecap hanging out right in between Cookie and Alex in the photo. I'd been so obsessed with what was going on up top that I'd never even let my eyes wander to the bottom of the image.

"Oh. My. God," I said, as the reality of this whole wasted week apart hit me. "But that night when we broke up—you were being so weird. You never denied cheating on me—"

"Flan, I would *never* cheat on you. But that night, you never brought cheating up once! I know that because I've had all week to torture myself memorizing every single thing you said." He ran his fingers through his hair. "Look, I know that night was weird.

Kennedy found me at that party and said all this stuff about overhearing you tell your friends that the pressure was on me to make Paris perfect and romantic for you." He paused and shot me an embarrassed look.

"What?" I asked, barely able to keep up with him.

"It's crazy, I know, and the look on your face makes me feel even stupider for believing her. But that's what I came over to talk to you about that night. Before I knew it, you were breaking up with me. Then I started getting texts from the guys saying what a great time you were having all over the world. I guess I just thought you were over it."

"Unbelievable," I said. "You should have seen the terrifying breakup specialist that SBB threatened to sic on me if I didn't get 'over it'—and I still couldn't even come close." I shook my head. "So then you sent the postcard—"

"I knew the postcard would come back to haunt me," Alex said, blushing. "So lame. I know. I just couldn't stand not talking to you. But I also didn't know what to say to you."

"Clearly," I joked, cutting the tension for the first time all week. It felt so good to be able to do the thing that came most naturally to us: laugh.

"You need to put down that hot dog now," Alex

said, taking it out of my hands and setting it on the bench beside me.

"Why—" I started to say, but before I knew it, Alex had swooped me up in a full-body hug. Our eyes locked.

"Because it's time to kiss and make up," he said, pressing his lips to mine.

Tingly feeling!

For a split second, I thought about the last time I'd been kissed—by Dave the Creeper on the beach in Sydney—but only for the sake of comparison between what a horrible kiss felt like and what the world's best kiss felt like. I forgot to breathe. I forgot to care that I was now sitting on my hot dog. I forgot everything about this entire wreck of a week. And when I opened my eyes, my prince was back.

"There's something I've been meaning to tell you for a while," he said softly, still holding me tight. "And for reasons I can't explain, this week I wanted to tell you even more than usual. And I really don't know when I started stammering so much but I guess I'm just nervous and—"

"Alex?"

"Flan?"

"Just say it," I said, feeling my heart race under my sequined Moschino cardigan.

Alex took a deep breath. He closed his eyes, then opened them.

"I love you," he said, with this incredibly endearing combination of nervousness and sincerity. I opened my mouth, wondering whether I was actually going to say the words that had been on the tip of my tongue since I first heard the name Alex Altfest, when Alex started speaking again.

"Oh, crap. I'm probably not supposed to say that right after we had this big fight. Now it sounds like I hadn't meant to say it all along. But I had. Did I blow it? Should I have waited to say it at some romantic time—?"

"Alex?"

"Flan?"

"Shut up."

"Shut up?"

"I mean . . ." I laughed. "Shut up, I . . . I love you too." I pulled him in for another kiss. "And for the record, I don't care what Kennedy says about Paris and romance and whatever—there is nothing more romantic than being right here, right now, with you."

We stood up, grinning, holding hands, and brushed the hot dog remains off our coats. This time, when we rejoined the scene on the street, I noticed all the beautiful things about the city. The rose vendors on the street, the click of horses leading carriage rides through the park. The sky had turned dark and all the city lights were glowing. We were glowing too.

"Our friends are going to freak out when we tell them," I said, squeezing Alex's hand in the cold.

"We should think of a fun way to surprise them," Alex agreed, buttoning up his coat. "How about tomorrow night?"

"Perfect," I said, as we kissed one last time—make that two, no, three last times—before parting ways.

Hmmm, I thought walking south on Fifth Avenue. Not technically closure, but I felt better about this convo than I'd ever felt about anything in my life.

Oh my God, was I really in love? I was really in love!

Now, all that was left was the gravy: relaying the good news to the girls, making up for lost time with Alex, and putting the whole Cookie Monsoon spring break debacle behind me.

Just then, I got a text from SBB. Leave it to my gladiatrix to make all of the above a reality. A very quickly approaching reality:

GREAT NEWS—JUST PILATE'D WITH AMBER . . . AND THE COOKIE FORMERLY KNOWN AS YOUR NEMESIS WAS THERE. CALL ME ASAP FOR DETAILS, BUT WE HAD HER

ALL WRONG. I ONLY WENT SLIGHTLY BALLISTIC ON HER BEFORE AMBER CONVINCED ME THAT SHE'S ACTUALLY AS SWEET AS HER NAMESAKE. SO CEASE AND DESIST GETTING OVER ALEX. AND PUT ON YOUR PARTY SHOES, PRINCESS—THIS CALLS FOR A CELEBRATION!

*A*nd . . . *go*," SBB shout-whispered, practically shoving Alex and me through the white double doors of the roof deck at the Peninsula Hotel. "Wait," she hissed. "Flan, come back! Your couture is crooked. You know what Eminem says—you only get one shot!"

It was Tuesday night, and the four of us—me, Alex, SBB, and . . . wait for it . . . Cookie Monsoon—had spent the last couple of hours chilling in the penthouse suite SBB had reserved for the night.

After we'd cleared up the massive misunderstanding yesterday, SBB had pounced on this last-minute opening at the Midtown hot spot and immediately invited everyone we knew to throw down at a mystery-themed party. She'd even sent out mystery invitations via messenger, without a return address, so none of the guests knew who the host was. As SBB said: it wasn't like New Yorkers knew why they ended up at half the parties they attended; this one would be totally memorable since its raison d'être would be unveiled during cocktail hour.

Only the four of us knew the real reason for the upscale gathering, and after SBB straightened the bow on the back of my sparkly red Jade Moodswing dress, and tightened Alex's paisley Hermès tie for the fourth time, we decided to give our little mystery one more toast.

"To the happy couple," SBB chirped, "who learned the hard way that whatever doesn't kill you makes you love each other. Awwww."

Alex winked at me and we clinked glasses of Perrier.

"And to Cookie Monsoon," SBB continued. "Object of *much* misdirected hate this week. Thank you for forgiving us, for being so cool, and for teaching me that amazing butt crunch move at Pilates yesterday. Have you considered patenting that yet?"

When Cookie laughed, her long layered Honora black pearl necklace jingled a little in the moonlight. She looked really gorgeous in a floor-length floral black silk gown, which last week I would have hated her for, but which this week only made me want to insist that she tell me where she shopped.

She turned to me. "I still can't believe this whole story. I swear, Kennedy was on my last nerve before this. But now I'm seriously going to have to delete her."

"The Lord taketh away, but then he giveth a replacement," SBB said, scratching her head. "Is that the way the saying goes? I swear, all this working out is turning me into a dumb jock."

"What SBB means," I said to Cookie, "is that now you'll have room in your phone to add new friends. Wait until you meet the rest of the girls."

"Speaking of which," Alex hinted, "SBB, are you ever going to let us out of here?"

"You're right!" SBB gushed. "You're the stars! You have get out there and unveil yourselves immediately!"

The penthouse doors were flung open, and the band to our left picked up their cue to start the drumroll. A spotlight shone right into my eyes, making me freeze temporarily, but the push from SBB told us we had better make our grand entrance . . . now.

"Good evening." SBB's voice was heard through a microphone. "May I present to you the reason you are all here at this party tonight. The city's most regal couple is back in business. Ladies and gentlemen, the Prince and Princess of New York!"

I couldn't see anything past the spotlight, but I could feel Alex's hand squeezing mine, and I could hear the initial gasps, followed by the loud cheers and applause from one particular corner of the party. Then I felt the frantic embrace of several pairs of arms and the curtain of some very long hair wrap around me.

The spotlight was lifted, and there were all my friends in a huddle around me. I looked behind me to see all of Alex's friends in a huddle around him, too. Everyone started talking at once.

"Okay, start from the beginning!" Morgan shouted.

"She took you back?" Jason said. "Even after that postcard?"

"Wait, was this whole week a hoax for you two to spend spring break alone?" Xander asked.

"Ahem, ahem," SBB boomed, back on the mic. "I think I can answer a lot of your questions by bringing out another surprise guest—the lovely and talented Cookie Monsoon!"

Again, a round of gasps flew around the circle. Those Thoney girls always had my back, even when they were slightly behind the gossip. SBB quickly rushed to Cookie's defense.

"Now before you pummel her—please don't

pummel her! Let me explain everything." She took a deep breath and I wondered how on earth she was going to sum all this up. Cookie was starting to look nervous in the spotlight.

"Long story short," SBB said. "Kennedy lied. Flan cried. Alex was fooled, and—as it turns out, Cookie rules! Thank you." She curtseyed. "Okay everyone, as you were. Party on!"

When the band picked up again, and the fringes of the party settled back into a comfortable buzz, my friends were still huddled around me with their jaws dropped.

"It's a long, stupid story, involving a doctored photograph and a series of misunderstandings," I started to explain. "The upshot is that Alex and I are back, and we're better than ever."

"I'm so confused," Camille said. "But you're happy?"

"Happy doesn't even begin to describe it," I said, glancing back at Alex with a grin. Half of me wanted to blab about the big step we'd taken yesterday at the park, but the other half felt this really special connection to him, just keeping it to myself.

"So wait, are we really allowed to like Cookie Monsoon now?" Morgan asked.

I nodded. "Absolutely."

"Good." Amory exhaled. "Because I must know where she got that dress!"

"Omigod," I said. "Me too. Hey, Cookie!" I called, motioning for her to join our group. "This is Camille, Harper, Amory, and Morgan. And we're all dying to know where you got that amazing dress."

"Oh, thanks," Cookie said, doing a modest little twirl. "It's Dries Van Noten. My boyfriend gave it to me for our two-year anniversary."

"Boyfriend?" I stammered. "Two-year anniversary?"

She laughed. "That's who I was visiting in Australia. I thought you met him at the barbecue. He was sitting right next to me the whole time. Another reason why this whole mistake is so ridiculous."

I clapped my hand to my forehead and had to laugh. "How self-absorbed was I that night that I didn't even notice you were with another guy?"

"On a self-absorbed scale of one to ten," a nasty voice hissed behind me, "I'd say you're usually about a fifteen."

I turned around to see Kennedy and Willa's glaring eyes.

"What are you doing here, Kennedy?" Camille said.

"We were *invited*." Willa flashed her invitation. "Who's behind this party, anyway?

"And *what* are you doing hanging out with these losers, Cookie?" Kennedy asked.

"I don't get it," I said, thinking aloud. "Why would SBB have invited you to our party?"

"Right on time!" SBB said, appearing behind Willa and Kennedy with a big grin on her face. "I invited them so I could have the pleasure of throwing them out! If I had to bulk up to bodyguard size, there was no way I was going miss out on doing something I've *always* wanted to do."

She grabbed Willa by the scruff of her Prada pea-coat. The rest of the crowd stood mesmerized as SBB literally lifted her off the ground. Immediately Willa started kicking and screaming, an unbecoming pose I'd already seen her strike too many times.

"Oh, hush," SBB cooed. "You're used to getting thrown out of clubs, and you know it never pays to put up a fight." She turned to glare at Kennedy. "Wait your turn—I'll be back for you."

When SBB came back to physically haul Kennedy toward the elevators too, SBB's personal bodyguard stepped toward her.

"Can I take them off your hands, Miss Benny?" he said.

"And deny me the pleasure of throwing them out myself? No way!" She laughed.

"This party sucks anyway," Kennedy belted out as the elevator door closed behind her and her fuming friend.

"Actually," Cookie said to the remaining partygoers in our bunch, "I think the only thing that sucked about this party just made an exit."

Alex put his arm around me and jerked his thumb at Cookie. "Oh, she's in." He laughed. "She's so in with you guys now."

As usual, Alex was right on point.

"Cookie Monsoon." I beamed, extending my hand. "Welcome to the in crowd."

Chapter 24

$\mathscr{C}$an I get two cheeseburgers with extra pickles, a coke, and a chocolate milkshake?" Alex said to a very jolly burger flipper at Burger Joint later that night. He turned to me. "Flan, what do you want?"

"All that was just for you?" I laughed.

"Hey." Alex pinched me. "So I didn't have much of an appetite this week. Obviously I have to celebrate its return with a good old double cheeseburger."

"I'll join you in celebrating and take two cheese-burgers myself," Xander piped up from behind us. Camille rolled her eyes but she was smiling.

It was ten fifty-nine on Tuesday night, and we'd made it just in time to catch last call at our favorite hole-in-the-wall burger joint—which was actually a hole in the side of the very fancy Parker Meridien Hotel.

SBB's mystery party wound down a little early because she had to catch a flight to Belize to support the kickoff of Jake Riverdale's South American tour for his new album, *River*. But the last hangers-on— me, Alex, Camille, Xander and . . . wait for it . . . Cookie—had decided to keep the party going.

It was amazing how immediately Cookie had been absorbed by our crew. After everyone got over the shock that they didn't have to hate her anymore, all it took was one look at her amazing dress, one friendly grin, a few crazy moves on the dance floor, and she was in. The best part was, Camille and I telepathied, homegirl knew how to late-night.

"What's better?" she asked, sticking her head between Camille's and mine. "The chocolate or vanilla milk shake?"

"Chocolate," Camille said.

"Vanilla," I said at the same time.

"Think they can make me a black-and-white?" she asked.

"Well, this *is* New York." I grinned.

Camille sighed contentedly, putting her arms around Xander. "Yes, only in New York can you start the night at the world's swankiest party, watch the world's biggest movie star throw out the world's biggest snobs by their ears, then end up with the world's best friends at the world's best burger joint—and still be home in time for the world's lamest curfew."

Xander laughed. "If you're ever trying to convince Camille's mom to extend that nasty curfew by a measly half and hour—I'd suggest *not* using the city-that-never-sleeps line. She was not a fan."

"Aw, Joan means well." I laughed, thinking back on all the times I'd been a little envious that Camille had one of those hovering-helicopter type of moms. "Remember the year she took us to watch the marathon and got so nervous we'd get trampled by the Nigerian runners that she actually tried to put leashes on us?"

We were cracking up as we took our burgers and shakes over to a booth in the corner. Alex and I shared a secret smile when we slid into the booth where he'd once written our initials on the heavily graffitied wall.

"What's that stars-in-your-eyes look about, Flan?" Camille said, teasing me.

Instead of admitting the embarrassing truth, which was that I was actually resisting the urge to pull out a pen from my bag to draw a heart around our initials, I said, "I guess I've just been thinking what a great night it was, and what an amazing city we live in. Think about it," I said, looking at my friends. "Between us, we've been all over the world this week—"

"Not Alex," Xander joked. "He's only been all around the loop in Central Park, moping!"

Alex knocked his friend on the shoulder and tossed a few fries in Xander's milk shake. "That's what you get for making fun of my pain." He laughed.

"Whatever, dude," Xander said, slurping up the milk shake and getting it all over his face. "That's how I like my fries anyway."

"Flan, you were saying?" Cookie interrupted, with that what-we-girls-have-to-put-up-with shake of her head.

Again, Camille and I exchanged telepathic glances. This girl was so like us, it was ridiculous.

"I was just saying, we've been all over the world—except for Alex." I patted his knee. "And I'm pretty sure we can still safely say there is no place like home."

A round of nods from Xander, Camille, and Cookie backed me up.

"That fancy French waiter looked at me like I was insane when I tried to dip my frites in my milk shake at his fancy French bistro," Xander said.

"And even though seeing Jade Moodswing's atelier in Paris was life changing—I think I can wait till she reopens her Chelsea shop this summer."

"The only complaint I have about this city is that until last week, I was hanging out with some pretty bad company," Cookie said, sounding more serious than I'd heard her. "But"—she quickly grinned—"something tells me that's not going to be a problem anymore."

I gave Cookie a big grin just as I felt Alex take my hand under the table.

"So," he said, "if you think New York's the place to be, maybe I shouldn't give you the gift I picked up today."

I looked at Camille and Xander, whose eyes both dropped down to their burgers, evidence that they were already in on whatever Alex had planned.

"What do you mean?" I asked quickly. "That's not fair!"

"Are you sure you want it, city girl?" he asked.

I bobbed my head, unable to stop grinning at him.

He reached into his pocket and pulled out a white envelope with my name on it. I slit it open and pulled out the card. On the outside was a picture of a pug and a Pomeranian nuzzling noses. OMG, I hadn't even *told* him about Noodles and Frances—who, by the way, had a doggie date next week. We were totally meant to be!

"Are you gonna open it or what?" Camille said.

Whoops. I opened the card, which said, *Let's never fight again.* And at the bottom, in Alex's hand, were those three thrilling words: *I love you—Alex.*

I was so focused on the note that I almost didn't notice the gift card inside. It was to McNally Jackson, my favorite independent bookstore on Prince Street. I'd spent whole afternoons browsing their shelves, and their café had the best blueberry scones in SoHo, but I was still a little confused. What did he mean about New York City?

"I couldn't stop thinking these past few days about how excited you were when you planned the GPA," Alex explained. "You made that *Guinness Book of World Records*–size binder and everything. And it stunk that you didn't get to see the payoff." He shrugged. "So I thought you could go to McNally and pick out some new travel books . . . because maybe you should start planning the weekend getaway I'm taking you on."

My jaw dropped. "Are you kidding?" I turned to Camille. "Is he kidding?"

"No way—and we're all going. Memorial Day weekend. All you have to do is pick the place and say jump, and we'll be on the plane."

"Oh my God, I get to pick the place?"

"That's the idea." Alex nodded.

"Because I have *always* wanted to go to Budapest. I hear they have this castle that's bigger than Central Park, and pierogies—you know I love pierogies!"

"This from the girl who was just raving that there's no place like New York," Xander teased.

"So you like your gift?" Alex asked, still squeezing my hand.

"Love," I said softly. "I love . . . my gift."

"What do you say, Cookie?" Camille said, swallowing the last bite of Xander's burger. "Are you in?"

"I say," Cookie said with a grin. "I say . . . Budapest or Bust!"

"Wow," I said. "I think you just gave us the anagram for our next trip: BOB!"

My instinct was to whip out my iPhone and start a preliminary notepad for BOB, but when Alex leaned across the table to kiss me on the cheek, I decided against scheming for the future and settled on swooning in the present.

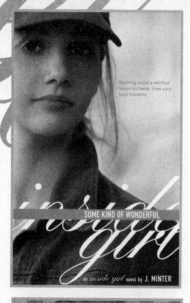

Find out how it all began in the Insiders series, also by J. Minter

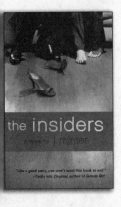

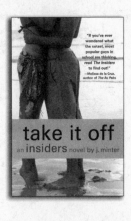
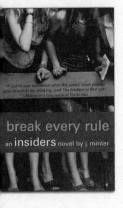